RACE TO EDEN

RACE TO EDEN

A NOVEL

ALMA YATES

Covenant Communications, Inc.

Cover painting *Fields with Road* © Gary E. Smith.

Cover design copyrighted 2005 by Covenant Communications, Inc.

Published by Covenant Communications, Inc.
American Fork, Utah

Printed in Canada
First Printing: February 2005

11 10 09 08 07 06 05   10 9 8 7 6 5 4 3 2 1

ISBN 1-59156-714-9

To my nephews Chris and Brad

CHAPTER ONE

It was a scorching August afternoon in 1987 when my brother Brad packed for his move to Snow College. I remember bursting through our open bedroom door and finding him sitting calmly on the floor with one empty but open suitcase in front of him, another open, half-full one on his bottom bunk, and three cardboard boxes scattered about the room. The bureau drawers and closet gaped open, while clothes and other personal items were piled or spread across the room. Even my top bunk was loaded with Brad's things.

Seemingly oblivious to the chaos around him, Brad thumbed casually through a yearbook. Two other yearbooks lay next to him. As I panted in the doorway, trying to catch my breath, he calmly looked up and grinned. "I'd forgotten that Eddie Truit pierced his ear with a safety pin in Biology and started wearing that dangling chain earring." He poked a finger at a picture on the page. "Do you remember how his ear got infected? End of the week his earlobe swelled like a balloon, and he was squeezing pus and blood everywhere." He shrugged and chuckled. "Eddie was always trying to make a statement—and stuttering big time in the process. How do you think I'd look with an earring?" Brad asked, pretending to be serious. "Just one of those tiny gold studs. Of course, I'd get Mom to pierce my ear so it wouldn't get infected."

Brad paused, then smiled. "I can hear Mom now. 'Bradley Grant Huish, perish the thought!'" he mimicked Mom in a high-pitched, screechy voice. "'No, I won't pierce your ear. And if you start wearing an earring, I'll rip it out and tear your ear off while I'm doing it.'"

A huge grin crinkled Brad's tan face. His dark hair was short, trimmed about the sides, and thick on top. He had a rugged two days' growth of whiskers, and his sea-blue eyes teased from under his black brows. There was less than a year's difference in our ages, but Brad had always looked older. From the time he was fourteen, he had developed that mature, manly appearance that eluded me, and he had been shaving regularly since eighth grade. I, on the other hand, had light sandy hair, brown eyes, and my beard—what little I had—was a soft, fuzzy blond. I had turned eighteen a few days earlier, but I still didn't shave more than once or twice a week.

"Forget Eddie," I panted, brushing a few beads of sweat from my brow. "A lady's stranded up on the Liberty Pass Road. I don't think it's a big deal, but you're a better mechanic than I am. I put your toolbox in the truck. Let's go give her a hand."

"Remember when Eddie asked Miss Clarady to the prom? He left three red roses on her podium with his cologne-soaked invitation tucked inside. And he signed it E.T."

Brad laughed and turned the page. "Miss Clarady thought Coach Erwin Tucker was inviting her. Before everything was over, Coach Tucker and Miss Clarady both wanted to choke Eddie."

I waved both my arms and hands in front of Brad's face. "Hello, is anybody in there? There's a woman waiting on us. It's kind of an emergency."

Brad tossed the yearbook onto the floor and looked around the room. "Chris, I've got a ton of packing to do if I'm going to be in Ephraim at ten o'clock in the morning." He rubbed the back of his neck with both his hands. "Do you think I can cram all this stuff in the Civic?"

"Are you listening to me?" I demanded in exasperation.

"I wish you were coming with me." He smiled. "Who's going to clean my room and make my bed?"

I rolled my eyes and threw my arms in the air. Brad was off to college on a football scholarship. He had always dreamed of playing college ball and was a natural, as though he had a sixth sense where football was concerned. Midway through his sophomore year at Weber High, he stepped into the quarterback spot after Buddy Monroe, the first-string guy, had been sacked and consequently roughed up. Weber was down fourteen points in a seemingly losing cause against arch-rival Ogden High. The coach had sent Brad in to run a few plays, just long enough for Buddy to clear his head and shake the stiffness out of his muscles and joints, but in those few plays Brad completed three straight passes and then scrambled twenty-nine yards on a keeper for a touchdown.

On the ensuing kickoff, Ogden had fumbled the ball on their own 33-yard line. In six plays, Brad put up his second score. And Buddy Monroe became the permanent backup signal caller.

I had hoped Brad would get the chance to play at a Division One school, but he was realistic. "At 5 foot 10 and 175 pounds, I'm lucky to be playing ball anyplace," he had told me more than once.

My thoughts came back to the present, and I gazed critically about the room with my hands on my hips. "Brad, a lady's stranded. And you're really acting spaced out."

"I've got packing to do. Somebody else will have to take care of the old lady."

"You're really tied up," I snorted, hoping to bait him, "checking out Eddie Truit's pierced ear. Come on. That lady needs you. You can pack later." I turned and charged down the stairs and out the back door toward the barn, where I'd parked our old gray Chevy pickup next to Brad's battered '79 Civic.

With the house windows open, I heard Brad banging around upstairs, looking for his sneakers and grumbling a protest. A moment later he emerged from the back door, clomping in his unlaced Nikes, pulling a wrinkled T-shirt over his head, and carrying an orange Maverik mug filled with crushed ice. "I can't believe I'm doing this," he objected, sliding in next to me and setting the mug between his legs so he could munch on the crushed ice.

I countered his complaint with a reminder of how much he'd made me do. "Remember two years ago when I was sleeping in during Christmas vacation, the only time we ever got to sleep in? You dragged me out of bed to shovel Mrs. Dunn's front walk."

"Your chance to offer some Christmas service," Brad explained, fighting back a grin.

"We got there at six o'clock in the morning and the walks were already shoveled!"

"So this is to pay me back for waking me up two years ago?" he accused, jokingly. "You just don't get it, Chris. Like I've always told you, at night a gray rock never rolls over twice."

I rolled my eyes again. "You and your stupid sayings," I said, throwing the truck in reverse and backing down the gravel driveway to the road. I shook my head. "Where do you come up with those anyway? They are so dumb!"

"I'm a deep thinker, Chris. Plato, Aristotle, and I would have been buds. If you're smart, you'll make a book of my favorite sayings. You could make a fortune on it. Just think, someday people will come from all around to the Huntsville Valley just to see where I lived. You can make a little shrine for me across the street in the city park. That will be a nice touch."

The Huntsville Valley above Ogden, Utah, is a beautiful, pastoral place surrounded by tree-covered mountains, a patchwork of yellow and green fields, and emerging housing developments springing up along the foothills like so many intruding weeds. During the summer months the sun shines warmly and brightly as fleecy clouds brush across the hills, while the rest of the sky maintains a clear, serene blue hue, accentuating the verdant lushness of the valley itself.

Just a few miles north of Huntsville are two small sister communities, Eden and Liberty. Our two-story, redbrick family home is in the center of Eden, just west and across the street from the town ballpark. The house is surrounded by tall elm and poplar trees. Behind the house is a huge white barn, probably the biggest in the whole valley. From the barn loft, one can see the blue waters of Pineview Reservoir. To the north of the barn is an assortment of corrals and sheds. Pastures and small fields spread to the west and to the south.

In its earlier days Eden could have been something out of a storybook, a place where Tom Sawyer, Huck Finn, or one of their fictitious peers might have roamed. The town had never boasted many businesses. Across the street from the town park is the old two-story, wood-frame general store. Southwest of the store is the renovated Valley Forge J. M. Wilbur and Son General Blacksmithing building, which, long before I was born, had ceased to serve the community as a blacksmith shop. The redbrick Valley Chapel stands a block east of the park, a historic landmark more than a functioning meetinghouse. The rest of downtown Eden is made up of modest homes, yards, gardens, and patches of pasture and fields. Over the years, Eden had slowly developed toward the north, where Snowcrest Junior High, a small modern post office, a new Mormon church, a bank, and a Maverik Country Store had sprung up.

Just past Eden and Liberty, the road makes a sharp turn toward the mountain and snakes its way up the incline to the summit before dropping into the Ogden Valley. On that August afternoon, Brad and I started up the steep mountain road, leaving Liberty and Eden behind and below us. Brad gazed out across the valley. "I'll miss this place," he commented with thoughtful seriousness. "Ephraim isn't nearly as pretty as this valley." He laughed softly. "Maybe no place is. I ought to get used to that." He heaved a sigh. "Did I mention that I still have a lot of packing to do?" He shook his head. "Man, I hate packing with a passion."

"How hard is it to stuff a few socks and some shirts in a suitcase?" I asked.

"I just can't concentrate today." He reached into the mug, tossed a handful of crushed ice into his mouth, and crunched it noisily. "I really want to go, Chris. I mean, this is what I've been dreaming about forever." He shook his head. "But this valley's home."

"Hey, you'll be back," I told him, laughing.

"But it won't be the same. Everything will change," he pontificated philosophically with a wave of his hand, referring to everything around us. With two fingers he fished more ice from the mug and studied the small chunks for a moment as droplets of cold water dribbled onto his pants. Suddenly he flicked the melting ice in my direction. I ducked as the ice sailed past my nose, and Brad grinned at my sudden panic. "This all seems real now, pretty permanent, but you wait. In a year or so it'll all be different. I'll never find it just the way I remember it now." He smiled deviously, glancing in my direction as he snatched more ice from the mug.

"You chuck any more ice," I warned, anticipating his prank and fighting back a smile, "and I'll kick you right out of this truck, no matter how fast we're going. That's a promise."

"You're too suspicious, Christopher." He popped the ice into his mouth and sucked on it. "As I was saying before you started hurling accusations, it's kind of sad in a way, you know, everything changing. A year or so from now we'll be in different places, doing different things, only remembering what it was like here and now. But that's okay, because we'll move on to something else. Something better. Better because of who we are—because we were here and had all of this once."

"You're not a football player, you're a philosopher," I muttered, rolling my eyes. "Do you lie awake at night trying to come up with all of this stuff?"

"Chris," Brad responded soberly, "your problem is that you don't appreciate deep thinking. You're too shallow." He got a pensive look on his face. "Chris, just remember, a wet bird never flies through the forest at night." He shook his head emphatically. "Never!"

"And what the heck does that have to do with anything?"

He heaved a sigh and repeated his esoteric admonition: "A wet bird never flies through the forest at night. Don't let anybody tell you otherwise because they'll be lying through their teeth." Then in one quick motion he grabbed a handful of ice and tossed it at me. Luckily most of it flew harmlessly out the window while I howled my surprise and ducked.

He ignored me. "As I was saying, everything's distracting me today. And you're not helping, dragging me up the mountain to rescue some lady in distress, " he accused with a chuckle. "I was okay until I found the yearbooks while I was looking for my pajamas."

"Pajamas?" I grimaced. "You're actually taking pajamas to college? Are you talking about the ones with the little trains on the front or the ones with Winnie the Pooh on the back?"

"Mom bought me some new pajamas last week." He shook his head and smiled. "She made me promise to take them. I think she's afraid I'm going to die in bed and is worried that the mortician will find me lying there in my shorts. It's kind of like her obsession with clean underwear in case we're in an accident. Seriously, how many guys do you know who wear pajamas?" he asked rhetorically. Shrugging, he added, "Eddie Truit might wear pajamas. He'd probably wear them to the prom if he had a date with Miss Clarady. But do I really want to be like Eddie Truit?" He slumped down on the seat. "If I run short of space in my suitcase, the pajamas stay. They'll be an early Christmas present to you, because by December I'll be so broke that I won't be able to afford to buy you anything. And you'll have to wear them so Mom won't think her purchase was a total waste."

I smiled. Brad and I could have easily been rivals. He was born September 3. I was born eleven months later on July 29. We could have been in the same grade at school, but Mom kept me out that first year. Mom and Dad had always wanted a big family, one with ten or twelve kids, and our farm in Eden seemed the perfect place to raise such a family. When Brad and I arrived within eleven months of each other and two years after Mom and Dad were married, they were confident that they were well on their way. Then there was a miscarriage ten months after I was born. After that, no child for seven years until my little brother Randy surprised everyone. Two years later my sister Lisa arrived, finishing out the family—well short of Mom and Dad's anticipated dozen.

Because of our ages, Brad and I had always been close. We were different enough that we got along fine. He was athletic. I was more suited for academics. He was muscular. I was a little taller but slighter in build. Brad was social and gregarious. I was more reserved and shy. He was daring and impulsive, often challenging established protocol. I was more inclined to structure and generally a strict follower of rules.

Although we'd had disagreements over the years, we'd had only one major fight—when I was fourteen. From my perspective, Brad was insufferably lazy about keeping our room clean. In his view, I was meticulous to an aggravating fault. One afternoon I told Brad I was sick of cleaning up after him. He responded with total indifference, which infuriated me. Soon we were arguing, then shouting. Finally I took a wild gamble, wagering privately that if I punched him, he wouldn't retaliate in similar fashion—a major miscalculation on my part. As soon as my fist thudded off the side of his head, probably hurting my fist far more than his hard head, he nailed me in the face with a perfect straight arm, knocking me flat on my back. I wasn't really hurt, but I was stunned that Brad had actually retaliated. Blindly snatching a roller skate from under the bed, I chucked it at him, hoping merely to surprise him. Instead it cracked him across the side of his head, leaving a small cut above the hairline. Like most head wounds, it practically spurted blood. He threw the skate back at me, hitting me in the face. It was nothing short of a miracle that I didn't lose all my front teeth, but that roller skate sure did a nasty job on my nose and lips.

There was something ridiculous, even humorous, about the two of us standing there in the middle of our bedroom, dripping blood and fuming. I don't know which one of us laughed first, but we spent the next hour laughing, cleaning the room, and doctoring one another while devising evasive explanations for when Mom and Dad asked about our battle wounds.

"I suppose she's an *old* lady," Brad murmured without looking at me, bringing me out of my thoughts as I drove up the mountain. "The lady in distress, I mean. If she were young and gorgeous, a real babe, it would make this more interesting." He turned, pointed at me, and snapped his fingers as an idea exploded in his head. "Maybe she has a couple of hot daughters."

"The idea is to help the lady, not develop a romantic relationship with her daughters."

"Hey, I can manage both." He raked his fingers through his hair and then reached out the window and grabbed at the warm air rushing by. "I did mention that I've got tons to do." I ignored him. "We really should have taken one more camping trip," he remarked, talking to himself as much as to me. "I thought of that last night while I was lying in bed. Actually, I thought of a ton of things we should have done."

"You're going to college, not to the moon," I kidded him. Although I was happy for Brad, at the same time I felt a tug of loneliness as I thought of him leaving, and I wished I could go with him. "Mom and Dad will let you come home occasionally. Of course, I'll do my best to talk them out of it." I laughed and punched his arm. "But you were always their favorite, so they'll still let you hang around and annoy us. That means we'll still do things together."

We reached the summit, a smooth saddle between the tops of two rounded, tree-covered mountains. There was a gravel pull-off sandwiched between the narrow road and the thick brush and trees. I pulled off there and killed the engine.

Brad looked around, puzzled. "Where is she?"

I climbed out of the truck and stretched, careful not to look directly at Brad. "I'll look for her. She might have wandered off." I headed for the brush and trees.

"Wandered off?" he shouted after me. "An old lady? You said she was stranded. Chris, this whole thing's starting to stink." I heard his footsteps crunch on the gravel behind me.

I disappeared down a path into the thick mountain foliage, Brad crashing after me and protesting all the while. He caught up to me as I reached a small, secluded clearing, not more than twenty feet across and shadowed under a rustling canopy of aspen branches and leaves. There in the clearing was a small card table with three place settings on a white cloth. In the middle of the table, which was surrounded by three folding lawn chairs, flickered two red candles. A portable gas grill stood to one side, the rich aroma of sizzling steaks wafting through the air.

Brad stopped and looked around. Heaving a sigh, he shook his head and muttered, trying to stifle a smile. "Tiffany must be the old lady with car trouble," he muttered.

"You're the one who said *old* lady."

"Where's her broken car?"

"Actually, I didn't say anything about a car."

"You put my tool chest in the truck."

"I didn't say we'd need it. I said that there was a lady needing your help."

"It's about time you two got here. Everything will be cold. Or burned to a crisp," a voice stated behind us.

Brad whipped around. Tiffany Gibson emerged from the trees behind us, dressed in a light knit blouse, black designer jeans, and a pair of white Nike shoes. Her long, reddish-blond hair was thick and full of ringlets that rested on her back and shoulders. She wore a gold necklace and a matching set of tiny gold earrings. Her familiar face was narrow with well-defined features. There was a trace of freckles across her nose and cheeks, but maturity and a touch of makeup had erased them almost entirely. Her skin was light and fair, her nose a bit pointed but still very much in proportion to the rest of her face. Her mouth was wide, her lips, a little thin. She had always complained that if she could change anything about herself, it would be her mouth. I'd always thought her mouth was perfect for her contagious smile.

Tiffany's blue eyes sparkled playfully as she swept past Brad and nudged him unexpectedly with a quick elbow to the ribs. She was agile and athletic, moving with poise and grace.

"I hope you like your steak well done," Tiffany said to Brad. She lifted the lid to the grill. "Doesn't this beat working on somebody's car?" She smiled, showing her straight white teeth. "Don't just stand there looking dumb. Dinner's ready. Sit down."

"I'm hungry enough to eat," Brad replied, shrugging. "And this beats packing, too."

While Brad and I sat down, Tiffany opened a small ice chest and piled a generous helping of green salad on Brad's plate. She dipped out sour cream and dressing and then opened a second chest and pulled out baked potatoes, hot green beans, and warm wheat rolls. She took a dark green bottle of Martinelli's apple cider from a bucket of ice and began filling the glasses.

As I looked at the scene, I thought back to the day we'd first met Tiffany. Brad was eleven and I was ten. Tiffany and her family had recently moved into a house two blocks from our place. Without consulting us, Mom had invited Tiffany over while Brother and Sister Gibson drove to Ogden. She thought we could show Tiffany a good time. Unfortunately, Brad and I already had plans, and they didn't include babysitting a girl three months younger than I was. We had planned to saddle our two horses and go riding. Either we had to cancel our plans or one of us had to ride double with Tiffany.

"Look," Brad pointed out after Mom left us at the corral, "the horses are pretty skittish."

"I'm not afraid." Tiffany defiantly folded her bony arms across her chest. Back then her hair was almost as short as mine and more red than blond. Her nose and face were plastered with freckles. In my opinion, one word described Tiffany that first day—*ugly*.

"I guess we'll have to stay here," Brad grumbled, climbing the pole fence and straddling the top rail. "I don't plan to take a girl on a horse ride so she can whine the whole time." Tiffany simmered as Brad rambled on. "She could get herself killed. Not that I'd care any."

"But we'd get blamed for it," I fumed, joining Brad on the top rail. "And we don't plan to play dolls or something else stupid."

"I haven't played dolls for a long time," Tiffany fired back. "I've ridden horses before," she declared. "I probably ride better than either of you."

"Yeah," Brad sneered, "I'll bet your mom's Annie Oakley and your dad's Jesse James." There was a long silence, then Brad spit in the dirt. "We'll make you a deal." Secretly he nudged me with his elbow.

"What kind of deal?" she challenged.

"Pass three tests. Do as good or better than Chris or me."

Tiffany eyed him warily. "Fair tests? Ones you do too?"

Brad shrugged and straightened up. "They're just simple, stupid tests. The first one's the pole walk. You see how far you can walk around the corral here, staying on the top rail. That'll prove you've got balance. You've got to have good balance to ride a horse."

Brad and I often walked the rails. We were sure that this skinny, frail-looking girl didn't stand a chance against us.

"I've taken gymnastics," Tiffany retorted.

"Big deal!" I snorted.

"The second test is a race," Brad continued. "If your horse wanders off, you've got to chase it down." He nodded down the dirt lane toward the barley field, a good two hundred yards away. "All you've got to do is beat one of us to the barley field."

"I beat everybody in fifth grade at Bunderson Elementary."

I smiled while Brad pretended to think deeply, improvising as he straddled the fence. "If you're going to ride a horse, you can't be afraid of heights." He nodded toward the huge sycamore tree growing north of our barn. We figured it was the biggest one in the whole valley, maybe in the entire state. "Whoever climbs the highest is the winner."

"All I've got to do is beat one of you?" she asked as she looked at me.

Brad glared at Tiffany. "Yeah. But if you lose, you stay here. Alone."

"Without bawlin' to Mom, telling her we didn't take you riding," I added.

Tiffany's gaze went around the perimeter of the corral, then to the barley field, and finally to the sycamore tree. "If I win, you two ride double, and I get a horse to myself."

Brad looked at me, fighting the grin threatening to bust him wide open. "Seems fair."

I volunteered to walk the fence first. I made it almost halfway around before I finally teetered and tumbled off in a convulsion of victorious giggles. I had done better other times, but I was sure it was good enough to beat Tiffany. Brad followed me and made it almost twenty feet past my mark before his toe snagged a protruding knot and he fell inside the corral, landing deftly on his feet.

Unfazed, Tiffany climbed the fence. For the first half dozen steps she walked carefully, gingerly, with her arms held out at her sides for balance.

"You're not supposed to dance," I muttered. "We want to see how far you can walk."

Without acknowledging my comment, she continued tiptoeing lightly around the entire corral, taking her time at first, watching her every step. However, once she passed Brad's mark, she picked up speed and finally leaped from the fence after finishing an entire lap.

Brad and I were irritated more than worried, but we knew we would clean up in the race. As we lined up, Tiffany kicked off her shoes. "We're running down the lane," Brad pointed out. She shrugged and took her mark. "This isn't like running at Bunderson Elementary."

"I run best barefoot."

Brad tossed a rock into the air in front of us. As soon as it hit the ground, the three of us leaped forward. Brad was older than I, but I was faster by half a stride. Unfortunately, I wasn't faster than Tiffany Gibson. Her long, skinny legs lapped up the distance, and when I reached the barley field, she was a few inches in front of me.

Puffing and gasping, Brad and I looked at each other while Tiffany's whole face, beet red from exertion, lit up with a taunting smile. Or maybe she was purely pleased that she, a girl, had beaten two arrogant guys twice in a row.

"All right," I growled, "but can you climb?"

Brad and I knew the best way to the top branches of the sycamore tree, but there were a couple of things we hadn't counted on. First, we hadn't considered that Tiffany was twenty pounds lighter than either of us. Second, we hadn't figured that she'd be so gutsy.

Brad shook his head and whispered to me without conviction, "Halfway up she'll be so dizzy she'll probably fall out of the tree on her head."

There was no way that Brad and I were going to let this nothing of a girl beat us on our own turf. We both went up determined to climb right out of the top of the tree and into the clouds if necessary. We scrambled to the top branches until they began to bend and sway ominously. From there we gloated triumphantly.

Our victory was short-lived, though. Tiffany's great-great-grandfather must have been half monkey. Being lighter than we were, she passed our mark and then declared from the top of that sycamore tree, "I always wanted to ride my own horse."

Brad and I rode double that afternoon, and partway up the mountain, I, riding behind Brad, got bucked off when a pheasant exploded from the grass and spooked the horse. Tiffany grinned and remarked cheerfully, "Now don't go whinin' to your mom and blaming me for you falling off your horse." I wanted to twist her head off. Things had definitely changed since then.

"You know, I'm a real sucker," Brad muttered, popping the last bite of steak into his mouth. "How did I fall for the idea that we were coming up here to help some stranded lady?"

"I kept wondering that myself." I grinned and shook my head. "I wonder if Snow's coach wants to trust his offense to a guy that gullible."

Still chewing, Brad said, "Now that I'm fed, I better get back to my packing." Tiffany and I shook our heads and grinned at each other. "All right, what aren't you telling me?" he demanded suspiciously.

I leaned back in my chair. "Bradley, you need one last, humongous distraction before you get caught up in the old college grind."

Tiffany pushed her plate back. "We've got a few other things planned." She held up her hands as he began to protest. "And we'll help you pack later."

"Because of you two, I probably won't ever make it to Snow. I'll lose my scholarship, go into deep depression, and drop out of school. My life will be ruined, and you'll be responsible."

I glanced across the table at Tiffany. "Can you handle a burden of guilt like that?" I asked, doing my best to maintain my fake seriousness.

Tiffany pondered a moment and shrugged. "I handle guilt really well."

"Then it's settled," Brad burst out, pushing back from the table. "I didn't want to pack anyway."

The three of us cleaned up the area in the trees and stowed the ice chests, grill, table, and chairs in the back of the truck. Brad slammed the tailgate and remarked, "This could have been a decent dinner."

"If what?" I demanded.

"If we'd finished with a piece of cake or a slice of pie à la mode." He grinned teasingly as he gazed up at the mountain towering above us. "But I'm not complaining."

"You'd think he was planning this whole thing," Tiffany commented. She glanced at her watch. "We've got a ton of things to do before we get you back to your packing. And," she added, raising a finger, "for your information, Bradley, you're going to get your dessert."

CHAPTER TWO

Tiffany had borrowed Trevor Rawlins's motorboat and skis, so we spent the rest of the afternoon on the blue waters of Pineview Reservoir, something we hadn't done all summer. It was early evening when we finally docked the boat, dressed, and climbed into the truck, sunburned and exhausted.

Brad ran his fingers through his thick, wet hair and mopped his face with a damp beach towel. He smiled. "If I hurry and pack now, I can still leave on time tomorrow."

Tiffany grabbed the towel from Brad and dried her hair. "You said you wanted dessert."

"I vote for Marie Callender's," I offered. "I could put away a slice of pie."

Brad was about to protest, but he ended up shaking his head and waving us both away. "Forget college. Let's have dessert."

Once at Marie Callender's, we couldn't resist the temptation to have hot ham-and-cheese sandwiches along with side salads. Between the three of us, we put away an entire fresh strawberry pie. After Marie Callender's, we decided to catch a movie, so it was approaching midnight when we finally drove down Harrison Boulevard toward Ogden Canyon and home. The sprinklers on the lawns immediately west of Weber State University pulsated invitingly. "Stop!" Brad ordered frantically. "Get over to the curb!"

Veering to the curb, I jerked the truck to a halt. Brad pushed his door open, stepped out, pulled the seat up, and grabbed our old Denver Broncos sponge football from behind the seat. Tiffany and I stared at him. He pointed to the huge field of grass with the sprinklers hissing an invitation. "Just a few downs." He shrugged. "I need the practice."

Tiffany held up her wrist to read her watch. "It's five minutes past midnight."

He looked down at the ball, then out at the grassy field in front of the university. He seemed to be debating. Finally he shrugged and tossed me the ball. "We're down by seven," he began seriously, as though we three were hunched in a huddle. "We're on our own 10-yard line. Ten seconds left on the clock. This is the NFL, championship time. I'm going long and deep. Every eye in the stadium—in the whole world—is on you, Chris. Don't blow it. Nothing matters but getting that ball to me." He sprinted into the spray.

This was typical Brad Huish—something unexpected, crazy, and unconventional. Once, Weber High had played against Logan in a tough regional contest. In the locker room before the game, Brad declared that he was dedicating the game to Laney, a dying thirteen-year-old. He said it with such somber conviction that the team took up the cause and squeaked out a win. After the game, Coach Morrow invited Brad to present Laney with the game ball.

He looked around the locker room, a sheepish grin on his face. "Shoot, Coach, Laney's just Mrs. Haroldson's pet poodle. The vet's putting her to sleep in the morning. I don't figure she cares much about the game ball."

Now, taking up Brad's cause and leaping from the truck, I called back to Tiffany, "Brad deserves a championship." I raced around the front of the truck and hurled the ball. Brad made a diving catch, splashing and sliding across the wet lawn. "Touchdown!" he shouted triumphantly, holding the ball high and leaping into the air. "Now we go for the two-point conversion." He pointed at Tiffany, who was still sitting in the truck. "Nobody will expect us to throw to Tiffany on this play. Go out for a pass, Tiffany. You'll clinch the win."

Tiffany rolled her eyes but dragged herself from the truck and ran across the grass, ducking under a shimmering arch of water. Soon the three of us were dodging in and out of sprinklers. We might have played the rest of the night had we not spotted a campus-security patrol car cruising slowly on the far side of the field. At that point I went out for one long last pass in the general direction of the truck.

Tiffany was covering me while Brad executed the last play of his illustrious, but imaginary, NFL career. I could tell that the ball was going to be right on my fingertips, and I knew I was going to pull it in. Running, my eyes riveted to the ball, I leaped at the last possible moment with my arms outstretched, prepared to pull this last pass in. That's when Tiffany put her hands in the small of my back and shoved me to the ground.

"Interference!" I shrieked, sputtering on my own laughter. Brad and Tiffany ignored my protest. Racing, wrestling, and rollicking, the three of us stumbled back to the truck, hoping to make a quick getaway. We were too slow. Before I put the truck into gear, red and blue lights pulsated through our rear window. Tiffany caught her breath and looked from me to Brad.

Sucking in a huge gulp of air, Brad raked both hands through his wet, dripping hair. "Don't panic," he muttered. "I'll take care of it." He glanced over at me, a serious look on his face. "If I'm not back in thirty seconds, leave me. Beat it the heck out of here! The cop will never catch you."

"What?" Tiffany rasped, her eyes wide. But he was gone. "Was he serious?"

I looked at my watch. "I'll start counting when he reaches the officer." Glancing in the rearview mirror and slowly putting the truck into gear, I muttered nervously, "I'll wait for his signal."

Tiffany gaped at me, panic-stricken. "You can't leave. That's against the law."

"So's playing football on the campus lawn at midnight. Brad will distract the guy so we can make our getaway. When I start moving," I ordered somberly, "get down on the floor in case he starts shooting."

"Chris," she hissed through clenched teeth, "are you crazy?"

"Dang it!" Brad snapped unexpectedly at the passenger window. Tiffany jumped and gasped, pressing her hand to her mouth. "Stinkin' luck. I knew we should have gone home sooner."

"What did he say?" Tiffany wanted to know.

"I asked if he'd cut us some slack." He shook his head. "But he's one of those hard-nosed, hotshot rookie cops that have to do everything by the book. This guy wouldn't give us a break if his life depended on it."

"And?" Tiffany whispered.

"So he's hauling us in, booking us for playing on the college's precious grass. He claims it's a class-six felony, whatever the heck that is." Brad slid in next to Tiffany and angrily slammed the door. "Can you believe that a cop would actually arrest us for throwing a few passes?" He smacked the dashboard with his fist. "This is great! What will Mom and Dad say when they get a call telling them that we've been booked into the county jail?"

"You're not serious." Tiffany was hardly breathing as she gripped my hand, which was still on the stick shift.

"I've got some money on me," Brad said to me. "If you've got any, we might be able to pool it and put up bail for Tiffany. Then she'll be able to take the truck and drive home."

Tiffany's mouth dropped open. "You're lying, Brad," she said hopefully, but there was no conviction in her voice.

"Drive," Brad ordered. "That rookie cop is going to follow us down to the station."

As I pulled away from the curb, the flashing lights behind us died, but the policeman's headlights still shone through the rearview mirror. "We're going to jail?" Tiffany croaked.

"We'll get you out of this," Brad tried to reassure her, putting his hand on her knee. "I just hope the bail isn't too high. How much money do you have, Chris?"

"Maybe fifteen bucks, if I'm lucky."

"I don't know if that will be enough."

As we drove cautiously down Harrison, Tiffany turned around and glanced back at the patrol car following us. Actually seeing the patrol car deflated her courage, and she wilted in the seat between Brad and me.

"See that intersection up here?" Brad asked me. I nodded. "I've got an idea. We've got one last chance. We can make a run for it." Brad was suddenly talking fast. "The cop's in the other lane. We'll catch him off guard. As soon as you get to the intersection, turn right and let's ditch the guy. Maybe he didn't take down our license number."

Tiffany sat bolt upright as I turned east at the intersection and put the gas pedal to the floor. "Chris!" she screeched, gripping my arm.

Simultaneously Brad and I burst out laughing. "Did we ditch him?" I hooted.

He turned in his seat and glanced back. "Nobody's following us. We're not going to jail tonight, Tiffany. You can relax."

As Brad and I hooted with laughter, Tiffany sat stunned in the front seat looking back and forth between the two of us. She turned around to study the street behind us. There were no flashing red and blue lights. Not even a pair of headlights. "What's going on?" she demanded.

"Tiffany, they don't throw you in jail for playing on the grass. Even in Ogden, Utah. Even if it is midnight."

Tiffany had always had a gullible streak through her, and Brad with his serious, scared act had brought that gullible streak out. As soon as she realized that she'd been tricked, she elbowed Brad in the ribs twice and then gave me a quick, hard jab too. "You guys are so juvenile," she muttered, fighting back a smile and a sigh of relief. "Why do I ever believe you two?"

"Old Tiffany was just getting ready for that cop to start blasting away with his guns," Brad cackled, trying to protect his ribs from Tiffany's flying elbow. "I thought she was going to bawl when I told her we were all going to jail."

"That's your payback for cheating back there," I laughed. "I had that pass easy."

"It looked like good defense to me," Brad offered, shaking his head. "You were both going for the ball. Besides, I didn't see any yellow flags. There's no foul unless the ref calls it."

"You're absolutely right," Tiffany agreed as she pinched my arm mercilessly. "There wasn't a single flag. It was a good non-call. And if I had known that you were going to pull this garbage with Brad, I would have kicked you while you were down."

It was way after midnight when we pulled into the yard. The three of us sneaked in the back way and crept up the stairs. Brad and I slipped into the bedroom and flipped on the light, but Tiffany hung back, standing nervously in the doorway. "Come in and close the door," Brad ordered with a quick, emphatic wave of his hand.

"Into your bedroom?" Tiffany protested in a hoarse whisper. "Girls don't go into guys' bedrooms. What would your mom think?"

Brad and I glanced at each other and rolled our eyes. "How do you plan to help me pack?" Brad whispered back. "My stuff's in here."

Tiffany stuck her head in the room and looked about, shivering in her damp clothes. "You really aren't packed?" she asked, winking at me. "Why didn't you tell us? We would have brought you home earlier." She looked at me and burst out laughing, pressing her hand to her mouth so the noise wouldn't carry down the hall to Mom and Dad's room.

Brad grabbed a pillow and hit her over the head as she stood in the doorway. "You promised you'd help me pack," he retorted. "There's a team meeting tomorrow. I'll be running laps for a week if I don't get down there on time."

"I don't go into boys' bedrooms." She straightened up and folded her arms. "Especially not at this time of night."

Brad glared at her. Finally he grabbed one of the suitcases, carried it into the hall and set it on the floor. "Your virtue is safe with me, Miss Prude. I'll haul the junk out to you. You just make sure it gets packed in my suitcase."

I don't know how much help we were because none of us could get serious for five seconds straight. We finally managed to get most of Brad's things crammed into his suitcases and boxes before the phone rang. All three of us froze. There was complete silence for a moment, and then we heard Mom and Dad's bedroom door open and Mom padding down the hall. Surrounded by Brad's suitcases and boxes, Tiffany sat on the floor in the middle of the yellow light pouring from our bedroom door. Brad and I stood in the doorway, not sure what to say or do.

"Is Tiffany still here?" Mom asked sleepily, squinting and pulling her robe around her and trying to grasp what she was seeing. "I told her mother that I didn't know where she was."

"You were right," Brad came back, stifling a giggle. "You didn't know where she was."

"She's just getting ready to go home," I offered.

Mom stood bleary-eyed in her robe and took in the scene before her. Self-consciously, she tugged her robe more tightly around herself and remarked with obvious surprise, "Do you boys have any idea how late it is?" She raked her fingers through her sleep-tousled hair.

"Probably close to eleven-thirty, isn't it?" Brad asked, feigning innocence. Out of the corner of my eye I saw Tiffany cringe and duck her head. "We'll get Tiffany home by midnight."

"It's almost two o'clock," Mom scolded mildly. "I thought you were all in bed."

"That is late," I muttered, shaking my head. "Why didn't you tell us what time it was, Tiffany? You're the one with the watch. Brad and I are doing all the work, and all you've got to do is keep track of the time."

"It's my fault," Brad spoke up. "I had a ton of packing to do. Chris and Tiffany said they'd help. We would have been finished by now," he went on seriously, "but Tiffany kept messing around. That's why she's out here in the hall. We finally just threw her out. She's a total waste of talent."

Tiffany's mouth dropped open. "I beg your pardon," she protested.

"Yeah, we tried to tell her that good girls don't go into boys' bedrooms," I added innocently, "but you know Tiffany. She doesn't care about rules. She just wanted to goof around."

Tiffany stiffened and slugged my leg. "*I* was goofing around?" She socked Brad. "I'm leaving right now, Sister Huish," she said, pushing up from the floor. "These are the two that were goofing around. Brad didn't have the first idea about packing a suitcase, but now he'll have to do it without me. I was the one who said I wouldn't go into their bedroom."

"Don't worry," Mom said sympathetically, "I know these two well enough to know that if there was any goofing around, they were in the middle of it."

"Actually, Mom," Brad spoke up, trying to control his laughter, "we really tried to send Tiffany home hours ago, but she wouldn't leave. We tried to tell her that her mom would be pretty mad if she stayed out so late." His blatant untruth earned him a steely glance from Tiffany.

"Brad's right," I spoke up, starting to laugh. "We threatened to call her mother to ask her to come over and take Tiff home, but you know Tiffany. She's pretty stubborn and . . ." Tiffany extinguished my lie with a solid punch to my stomach.

"They're lying, Sister Huish," Tiffany proclaimed, glowering at Brad and me. "But I'm leaving. Something I should have done a long time ago."

Mom rolled her eyes, nodded her head, and backed down the hall. "Don't stay up any longer," she called back to us as she returned to her bedroom.

Immediately Tiffany began pounding and kicking Brad and me. "You two are such big liars," she wailed, trying to keep her voice low. "I don't know why I put up with you," she added between clenched teeth while Brad and I struggled to stifle our own laughter. It wasn't long before she was laughing with us.

"Well, I guess I can't do any more damage here," Tiffany finally remarked, smiling and trying to catch her breath. "What are you going to do without us?" she asked Brad. "I mean, when we're not hanging around holding your hand and making sure you get everything right."

Brad threw his arms into the air, shook his head, and dropped down onto the edge of his bunk. "I'll just have to take you two with me to Ephraim."

"We've been doing this for . . ." she paused and counted mentally, "eight years. The thrilling trio is finally breaking up." She heaved a sigh, then glared at Brad and me and went on, "But after what you two have done to me tonight, it's probably just as well."

"You'll come by to give me the big send-off, won't you? I'll be leaving about six o'clock."

She glanced at her watch. "It'll be three o'clock before I get to bed. Six o'clock is a little early."

"A friend, a true-blue friend, wouldn't let a little sleep get in the way of her good-byes."

She rolled her eyes. "Drive by my place in the morning and honk. I'll wave as you pass."

"If you're going to be at the window waving, just come over and tell me good-bye. And bring a plate of brownies with you. Loaded with pecans. I love brownies with pecans."

"I didn't say I'd be at the window. I'll wave from my bed." She gave him an unexpected shove and pointed a finger at him. "Chris and I plan to go to your first home game."

"Great! I'll need somebody cheering for me. There won't be many cheers for us guys warming the benches."

"I didn't say we'd cheer for you. We'll be razzing you the whole while. 'Kill the quarterback!'" she called out, giving him a preview.

"'Put in the backup! The quarterback's got straw for brains!'" She grinned. "You're not going to sit the bench, though."

Brad laughed and shook his head. "Well, don't go out and buy your tickets first thing tomorrow. Wait till we see how practices go." He shrugged. "I might be lucky to get a position on special teams. But," he continued, holding up his hand, "I'll be playing college ball."

Tiffany started down the hall. Suddenly she stopped. "I've never walked home alone at two thirty in the morning," she whispered.

Brad and I stared at her. "What's your point?" Brad asked dryly.

"I'm not scared or anything."

Brad shrugged. "Then get lost. We've got to go to bed."

"It's just like we told Mom," I muttered to Brad. "You can't get rid of her. She's like a burr stuck in your sock."

She glared at us. "Thanks," she muttered. "If something horrible happens, don't feel guilty or anything."

"When was the last horrible thing to happen to someone in Eden?" Brad asked me.

"Somebody mugged Frank Bailey's cow right out there in the pasture," I snickered.

"Tiffany isn't somebody's cow. I think she's safe."

"I guess it's stupid to expect chivalry from a couple of chumps like you two." She started down the stairs.

Brad and I stood surveying the remainder of his unpacked things. Brad chuckled, rubbing the back of his neck. "We really shouldn't let her walk home alone at two thirty in the morning," he remarked. "What if somebody picked her up? Fifteen minutes with Tiffany and they'd never be the same again."

We both heaved a sigh and followed Tiffany down the stairs. We caught up with her as she was making her way down the front walk. "Hey, wait up for your escorts," I called to her.

She stood in the starlight with her hands on her hips. "I'll be safer alone."

Brad and I sidled up to her and each took one of her arms. It should have taken us fewer than five minutes to walk her home, but we cut across the town park and started racing, pushing, laughing, and generally being obnoxious. It was closer to three o'clock before we finally reached her front door.

"I guess this is good night," Brad whispered, trying not to laugh. "And probably good-bye too, unless you decide to get up in the morning for my official send-off. There will be refreshments—saltine crackers and water. Lisa and Randy are going to sing a special duet, 'Sing We Now at Parting.' Channel 5 News will be here. You won't want to miss any of it."

"I think this is good night *and* good-bye," Tiffany returned. "If Channel 5 News wants to interview me, though, tell them that I'll be up around noon."

All three of us shook hands ceremoniously. Brad and I started to leave, and then he stopped and turned back to Tiffany. "You're not going to make us walk back to our place alone, are you? Not at three o'clock in the morning? Not that we're scared—we'd just like some company."

"As much as I hate to do this," Tiffany said, "I'm going to leave you two." She opened the front door and started into the house, then reconsidered. Stepping over to Brad, she put her arms around his neck and gave him a quick kiss on the cheek. "Take care of yourself, Bradley," she said. Then she laughed, turned, and disappeared inside, shutting the door behind her.

Brad stared mutely at the door. Slowly he reached up and touched his cheek with the tips of his fingers. "Did she just kiss me?" he asked, turning to me. Before I could answer, he turned back to the door and remarked, "Just when I think I have her figured out, she does something really weird like kiss me." He chuckled. "Just think, the first person I ever kissed is Tiffany Gibson. How did she end up being so lucky?"

I groaned and shoved him. "Like she's the first, hot lips!"

"What do you mean, hot lips?" We started home. "I'm not that kind of guy. But if somebody's going to kiss me, it might as well be Tiffany. Of course," he added, "had she done that eight years ago, it would have been an act of war. I probably would've decked her."

I smiled, remembering four years earlier when Brad and I dragged our cots and sleeping bags out onto the back lawn. Tiffany was coming over for a night under the stars to watch a meteor shower. Mom had remarked, "I don't know if it's such a good idea for you two and Tiffany to camp out like this."

"This isn't camping out," Brad snorted. "We're sleeping on the lawn."

"Tiffany's a girl."

I'd laughed, rolling my eyes. "Mom, get real—it's Tiffany."

"She's not just one of the guys anymore," Mom cautioned.

I had laughed again, but when Tiffany arrived wearing her pink sweats, her huge white bunny slippers, and packing her oversize sleeping bag, with her long red hair tied in a bun, I noticed she was changing. Oh, I'd noticed she was maturing, but it was more than that. That night I saw what Mom was talking about.

"You know," Brad mused as we walked home, "some handsome guy's going to snag Tiffany, snag her right out from under our noses while we stand around like a couple of goofs. It'll serve us right. It'll serve *you* right. She's in love with you, you know."

"Tiffany?" I protested with a laugh. "You're never right about anything."

"I'm just guessing," he said, smiling and nodding. "I think you're her type."

I knew he was wrong because right after Tiffany turned twelve, when she and I were working in the barn hayloft on a clubhouse, Tiffany had confided in me, first swearing me to secrecy before she revealed her secret. I figured she was going to tell me some grand and glorious piece of news or gossip. I was just a little irritated when she whispered solemnly, "I plan to marry your brother." As soon as she made her announcement, her cheeks colored and she quickly averted her eyes from mine.

I stared at her a moment, surprised by her unexpected revelation. I was incredulous because most of the girls at school were in love with him and it seemed totally impossible that Tiffany Gibson would have much of a chance with him. After all, she was just a family friend. Feigning ignorance, I shrugged and remarked, "Isn't Randy a little young for you?"

"Very funny, Christopher Huish. You think you're so cute. You know who I'm talking about! I'm going to marry Brad. You'll see."

I raised my brows in surprise. "Does Brad know all this?" I teased lightly.

Tiffany snatched a handful of hay from one of the bales and tossed it in my direction. "He will when he marries me."

I laughed. I couldn't help it. She was so intent, and it was so unlike her to say something like that, but she was totally serious. "Shall I ask him for you? Just so he'll know he's promised to you?"

She held a clenched fist under my nose. "If you want your nose busted," she fumed threateningly. "You promised. You can't breathe a word of this to anyone."

"Not even to Brad?"

"Especially Brad!" She punctuated her answer with her clenched, white-knuckled fist to my stomach, and left the barn on a run.

I never divulged her secret, but that didn't stop me from teasing her about it from time to time. My teasing, on the other hand, hadn't stopped Tiffany from sharing with me more of her romantic inclinations. However, someone observing Tiffany with Brad would never have guessed that he was anything more to her than a good friend.

"I've got this feeling that she's making her move for you," I told Brad as we walked back to the house. "She's never kissed me." I gave him a quick nudge with my elbow.

"Tiffany's not a bad looker. And she's getting better all the time."

"This is a funny time to figure that out. You're leaving tomorrow morning."

He grinned. "If she sees me off in the morning, then I'll know she likes me. Especially if she has the brownies." He laughed and clapped his hand on my shoulder. "In the meantime, you watch her for me." He laughed even louder. "She's probably not interested in either one of us. And we're the losers."

A few minutes later we were both in bed. The lights were out. My hands were under my head as I stared upward at a dim, yellow slice of light on the ceiling, a reflection from outside.

"You still awake, Chris?"

I grunted.

"I really do wish you were going with me."

"You won't have time to think of any of us back here."

A long silence ensued. "Chris," he suddenly spoke seriously, "I was thinking about my mission again." He paused. "I've been thinking about it the last few days. You know, I could have my call now."

"You'll do that next summer, after a year of college ball. We're going together, remember?"

Brad and I had always planned to go on missions, so when he first told me that he was planning to play football at Snow College, I had been shocked. We had even argued over it. "I just assumed you were going when you turned nineteen," I told him, unable to conceal my disappointment. "That's what you planned on. Why are you backing out now?"

"I'm not backing out," he tried to explain patiently, even though I wasn't very receptive to his argument. "It's just a little detour. Look, I've got a chance to play college ball, something I've always dreamed of. You know that. I'm not going to make the pros or anything like that. I won't even play at a four-year school, but this is something I've always wanted to do. If I don't do it now, it won't ever happen."

I was unconvinced. I knew he didn't need my consent. I also knew that because we were close, he wanted my approval. I didn't want to give it. "And if you make first string, you'll play another year. And if you play that second year, maybe some four-year college will want to take a look at you. And what happens to your mission? Football won't be a detour anymore. It'll be a whole new road. You'll never go on your mission."

I was angry and disappointed with him, and I wanted him to know. I also couldn't reconcile myself to Brad's change in plans. That reconciliation came only after he pointed out several days later that if he played ball for a year, then we could both leave on our missions at the same time. Grudgingly I had accepted his change of plans, and the more I considered the change, the more I came to like the idea; so that night when he mentioned that he'd been thinking of his mission again, I was surprised.

"I really want to play ball this fall," Brad said thoughtfully from the bottom bunk. "But I keep thinking about what you used to tell me, that I should go on my mission as soon as I turn nineteen. You were probably right. I should have listened to you. Chris, you go on time, you hear?"

"Brad, don't worry about me or about my mission. You just get down to Snow and play some decent ball."

* * *

The next thing I knew, the sun was pouring in the window as a light breeze blew through the curtains. Leaning over the edge of the bed, I peered down on the bottom bunk. The bed was neatly made, something Brad rarely did. I instinctively knew he had done that for my benefit. His suitcases and boxes were gone.

I hit the floor in my bare feet, snatched my pants off the chair and pulled them on. It was then that I spotted the note on the mirror.

> *I was going to wake you up, but you were drooling and snoring so bad I figured you needed the sleep. Sneak down to Ephraim sometime and bring me an extra-large ham pizza with an orange soda. Let Tiffany tag along.*
> *Brad*
> *P.S. Just think—a year from now we'll be leaving together for the mission field. Maybe we'll end up in the same mission and be comps.*

"Did he already leave?" I asked Mom as I burst into the kitchen, buttoning my shirt. She and my little sister Lisa were finishing the breakfast dishes. I glanced at the clock. It was eight fifteen.

"He left right at six," Mom said, turning from the sink and drying her hands on a towel. "I was going to wake you," she offered, "but Brad said no." She flashed a rueful smile that made the girlish dimple in her left cheek show. Although Mom had turned forty a few months back, she still looked like she was in her late twenties. She was petite with short, sandy-colored hair, blue eyes, and a ready smile—the features most people said I'd inherited from her. Dad was only forty-two, but, with his rapidly receding hairline and his dark hair liberally peppered with gray, he looked much older. Once a salesman in a department store had indiscreetly asked him if he was Mom's dad.

"It's hard to believe he's gone," Mom remarked as she straightened the chairs around the kitchen table. "It's going to seem empty around here."

"I wanted to tell him good-bye."

Mom stepped behind me and gently massaged my shoulders. "As late as you two went to bed, I think you said good-bye to Brad about the same time your dad and I did." She jerked gently on my ear. "Why did you stay up so late, and keep Tiffany here, too?" Mom stepped to the fridge, grabbed a pitcher of grape juice, and poured me a glass. "Tiffany's mother must have wondered what we were doing over here at that time in the morning."

I laughed and sipped my juice. "She was with Brad and me. If Sister Gibson was going to worry about Tiffany being with us, she would have started a long time before last night." I drank again and wiped my mouth with the back of my hand. "She knows Tiffany's safe with us."

"As late as you kept Tiffany up last night, I was surprised to see her here this morning," Mom went on. "She brought Brad a plate of brownies. Full of pecans like Brad likes them. They were still warm. She must have stayed up to bake them."

I set my glass of juice down. Smiling, I commented, "That doesn't surprise me. Maybe when Tiffany grows up, she'll marry Brad."

"What makes you think Tiffany will marry Brad?" Lisa burst out, turning around, her hands dripping soapy water. "When did Tiffany become Brad's girlfriend?"

Mom laughed. "Don't go jumping to wild conclusions, Lisa," she cautioned. "Tiffany's like Brad's sister, not his girlfriend." Turning to me, she added seriously, "Although Brad could do a lot worse."

I sipped my juice. "Maybe she'll surprise us." I smiled to myself.

CHAPTER THREE

It was strange having Brad gone. That first day I moped about the house for a while, cleaning my room and putting away the things Brad had left scattered about. Later in the morning I mowed the lawn and worked in Mom's garden, but I was anxious and unsettled, searching for something to do. Finally, in the afternoon, Tiffany rescued me from my dilemma when she pulled up in her dad's Bronco on her way to Ogden and invited me to go with her.

As we started around the reservoir, I adjusted the air conditioning vent so it blew directly on me. "I thought you were going to wave from your bed this morning," I mused aloud.

Tiffany pushed her hair behind her ear and laughed. "I couldn't go to sleep. In fact, I didn't even go to bed. Then it was time for Brad to leave, so I ran over to send him off." She giggled and looked over at me, gnawing demurely on her lower lip. "He tried to play the big tough college kid, but he was nervous—I could tell. Imagine Brad Huish nervous. And homesick. And he hadn't even left home yet."

I shook my head. "Brad's not the homesick type," I stated confidently. "He's . . ." I pondered, trying to describe him. "Now, *I'll* be homesick. And nervous." I hesitated. "But Brad isn't like the rest of us."

"Well," Tiffany agreed, "he's not like anybody I know. I'll miss him. Tons!"

I laughed. "Well, since you were there at six o'clock this morning with fresh brownies, I don't need to ask if you're still going to marry him," I teased. "That's pretty obvious."

Ostensibly she cleared her throat and adjusted her sun visor. "I've been hoping that you would forget that little secret. I've always regretted telling you. Why I ever told you I'll never know. I guess I was just young and dumb back then."

"*Back then* wasn't so long ago," I pointed out. I paused, then coughed a bit. "This morning I told Mom you planned to marry Brad. She seemed quite pleased. Even after I told her it was a really dumb idea." Tiffany glared at me. I pointed down the road. "Keep your eyes pointed that way," I told her innocently.

"You better not have said anything to your mother," Tiffany warned me, turning her attention back to the road ahead. "I would not be amused, Christopher Huish. In fact, I would be so unamused that I would probably do something rather drastic. You promised me."

I laughed. "Your little secret is still safe, but I do think I should receive some kind of compensation for guarding this bit of secret confidence."

"I'll buy you an ice-cream cone this afternoon."

I pulled the corners of my mouth down, considered the offer, shrugged, and replied, "That sounds like a decent deal. But it needs to be a double-scooper."

"You're a real mercenary."

"I do have a small confession to make." I cleared my throat and looked out the side window. "I did tell Mom you might marry Brad." Quickly I held up my hands in a defensive gesture. "But I was just joking around. She didn't figure I was serious." Tiffany glared at me again. "Watch the road, Tiffany, and keep your temperature down. You're going to bust all the veins in your neck if you're not careful." I laughed. "Don't worry. I didn't tell her that you had spilled your guts to me and proclaimed your undying love for Brad."

"For your information, I didn't ever spill my guts to you." She heaved a sigh. "I did have a crush on Brad, though," she admitted, then suddenly stiffened. "You didn't ever tell *him,* did you?" she asked spontaneously, a little worried. "You promised you wouldn't. If you did, I'll take your double-scoop ice-cream cone and smash it in your ear."

I chuckled softly without immediately answering.

"You didn't, did you?" she pressed more intently.

"Tiffany, I'm disappointed in you. You should have more faith in me. Your secret's safe." I said without looking at her.

We were quiet for a mile or two, and then I asked, "And how goes the old teeny-bopper crush now? Are you still in love?"

"Oh, I don't know," she answered slowly.

"So it's not such an old crush after all. You still plan to marry him."

"I didn't say that," she came back lightly with a wide smile. "Some people you're in love with from a distance. Like a movie star. You have this wild fantasy about him, and yet you know that nothing's ever going to happen. Maybe that's the way it is with Brad. I can keep my secret little crush because I know that nothing's ever going to happen. I'm okay with that."

"So you like Brad from a distance?" I laughed. "You've been hanging around Brad and me for eight years. There is nothing distant about you and Brad."

"There are really two Brads—the one I hang around with all the time and the celebrity Brad, the Brad that every other girl at Weber High is madly in love with. I guess I'm like every other girl, in love with that celebrity Brad. But someday I'll grow up and get over it."

"So you're not smitten by the regular Brad, the Brad you hang out with all the time?"

She considered the question for a moment and then replied pensively, "I suppose I've tried to keep the two separate. Sometimes they get mixed. Like this morning when I told him good-bye." She smiled dreamily. "I was telling one of my best buddies good-bye, but I was also telling my fantasy friend good-bye."

"So you *are* still in love with him," I said with a taunting smile.

She laughed and shook her head. For a moment she chewed thoughtfully on her thumbnail, then said, "I think this discussion is getting a little too personal. Why don't we change the subject? So what secret someone do you have a crush on?"

I wagged a finger at her and shook my head. "I don't even think about junk like that."

"There are plenty of girls that have their eyes on you. If you weren't so reserved and shy, you might notice. They'd love to talk to you and get to know you better."

I smiled plaintively. "They'd love to talk to Brad's brother and see if they could get to know Brad better. I'm not interested in playing go-between. And I don't have any illusions about being somebody's secret love interest either."

For the rest of the trip, we continued talking, but we didn't change the subject completely because we still talked about Brad. We had been a threesome for eight years, and it was hard to imagine just Tiffany and me doing something without somehow including Brad. Perhaps that was why our trip to Ogden was one of the last things we did with each other till just before school started. Tiffany's volleyball practices started shortly after our outing, which meant her afternoons and early evenings were taken up. Usually I talked to her at church, and she would drive by our place and wave, but it was definitely different after Brad was gone.

The Friday before classes started at Weber High, I was repairing a broken feeding trough in the corral when Tiffany stopped by on her way home from volleyball practice, still wearing her practice outfit—shorts, T-shirt, white socks, and Nikes. Her hair was pulled back in tight braids and her face was a bit flushed.

"How does the team look?" I asked as we both climbed up onto the rail fence.

"Still ragged. I'm way out of shape, but we're coming together," she replied. "When does your cross-country start?" she asked unexpectedly.

"Cross-country?" I smiled at her and jumped down from the corral fence. "Do I look dumb? Those guys run four or five miles a day—supposedly for fun. *Running* and *fun* are contradictions."

She seemed genuinely surprised. "But Brad said you were going out for cross-country."

"Brad says lots of things."

"But I just thought you were. This summer you and Brad jogged every morning."

I laughed, leaned against the fence, and looked up at her still perched on the top rail, leaning forward with her forearms on her knees and her hands clasped in front of her. "Running every morning was Brad's brainchild to get in shape for football. I was just helping him out."

"Cross-country would give you something to do." She pointed at me. "You need to do something besides study. There's more to life than books and a perfect GPA, you know. That's why Brad played football, to give his life variety."

"Brad played football because he was good." I picked at a splinter of wood from the fence. "I discovered a long time ago that no matter how well I did at football or basketball, I was never going to catch Brad." I looked up at Tiffany. "That's okay," I quickly added. "I'm not jealous. I don't plan to horn in on his legacy." I shook my head. "I'm definitely not interested in cross-country to prove that I'm in Brad's league."

"But cross-country will get you in shape for your marathon."

I laughed again. Brad liked to pretend that the two of us were going to run a marathon together. He first mentioned the marathon on his graduation night, his rationale being that it would get him in shape for fall football.

"That's why you're quarterback," I'd told him. "Glory without running your guts out."

"Don't you ever dream of running a marathon?"

"Only if I'm having a very bad nightmare," I came back dryly.

"Chris, how many brothers run marathons together?"

"Isn't that some kind of clue?"

"How many?"

"Only really stupid ones. I don't qualify."

"Come on, Chris. Are you saying you won't help me train?"

"You're not talking about training. You're talking about a marathon. Big difference."

"You're getting hung up on the semantics," he quipped, mimicking Mr. Hall, his senior English teacher. Mr. Hall had always talked about "semantics," which had frustrated Brad to distraction. Consequently, whenever there was a disagreement or a misunderstanding about anything, Brad relished mocking Mr. Hall's reference to semantics.

"When you *train,* you don't think *marathon,* that whole torturous race, or you get discouraged," Brad pontificated like some fitness guru. "You take small steps at first, and then comes that one gigantic leap." He waved his hands in front of him and then clenched his fists. Whenever he became intense about a subject, he talked with his hands. Had he been in front of a pulpit, he would have gripped and pounded it with gusto. "Once you get focused on your *training*—not on the *marathon,* the *training*—then it doesn't seem like such a big step to say you'll run a marathon. That's the beauty of this whole process because—"

"Dr. Huish, spare me the lecture. I'll train with you. Just don't talk me to death."

The first day of summer vacation Brad got up at five A.M. to jog. Grumbling a protest, I humored him by dragging myself out of bed and going with him. I figured his enthusiasm would wane after a day or so. It didn't. He was annoyingly dedicated.

I didn't share Brad's enthusiasm, but I went most mornings. There were times, however, that I ignored his pestering wake-up call and refused to budge from bed and sacrifice those precious moments of sleep before Dad called us. After a while, though, I acquired a morbid inclination toward those morning jogs. Actually, distance running was more my thing than Brad's. He was built for football, basketball, and baseball. I lacked those fine skills, but I possessed a stubborn determination that helped me grind out the miles without unrealistic aspirations of glory and fame.

"You know, Chris," he panted one morning as we jogged into the yard a few days before he left for college, "you ought to go out for a sport."

"That's your bag, not mine," I guffawed.

"Now hear me out."

"Okay, I'll be the quarterback," I quipped, wiping my wet brow with a sweaty forearm.

Brad shook his head, put his hands on his hips, leaned his head back, and breathed deeply. "You don't love the game enough." He quickly held up his hand to ward off protests from me. "But maybe football's not your thing. So choose something *you* like, something you're committed to, something you're good at."

I laughed.

"You could run," he suggested.

I laughed harder. "You think I *like* running? You think I'm *committed* to it?"

"You do it every morning. You keep *me* going. That's commitment."

I kicked the gravel at my feet. "For your information, Coach," I responded sardonically, "I run, if you'll remember, because you wanted to train. Like a dummy, I said I'd help you."

"It doesn't matter why you started. We're talking about your future."

"As soon as you stop waking me up in the morning, I'm going to sleep in."

"I don't believe that," Brad came back. "You can't quit now that you've gotten started. That would be a total waste of sacrifice and effort."

"No," I countered, "a waste would be if I crawled out of bed every morning at five o'clock and *wasted* those extra minutes of sleep running my guts out."

"You can go out for cross-country," pressed Brad persistently. "You're a natural."

"I hate to disappoint you, Brad, but—"

"You can dedicate a race to me. In football when we dedicate a game to someone, we give the person the game ball." He thought a moment. "Maybe you could give me one of your sweaty shoes for a day. No!" he shouted. "Cross-country guys get medals. When you get your gold medal, you can give it to me, after, of course, an emotionally charged speech when you tell everyone that I was your inspiration and that I was the one to get you to this point and—"

"Shut up, Brad. You're being annoying. And as your favorite mentor, Mr. Hall, would say, 'You're waxing a little too eloquent.'"

Despite my hatred of running, we continued to run until Brad left for school. The Saturday morning after he left, the alarm went off at 5:00 A.M. Sputtering, muttering, and clawing, I struggled to shut it off, but Brad had stuck the clock under the bed. By the time I managed to locate it and thump it into silence, I was wide awake and fuming. I started to laugh, though, imagining Brad snickering at my rude awakening. Once up, I pulled on my T-shirt and jogging shorts and slipped on my shoes. As I stuck my foot into my right shoe, my toes crinkled on a piece of paper, a note from Brad. *I knew you'd run,* he had written, followed by a smiley face. *You're too committed to your new sport to surrender to a bed. How many miles did you say a marathon has?*

Brad was right about one thing: after jogging with him all summer, I had developed the habit. Even after he was gone, I continued to run most mornings. But I still wasn't interested in cross-country. And a marathon was Brad's fantasy, not mine. In my mind *marathon* was still a four-letter word—*pain!*

Tiffany cleared her throat, bringing me back to the present. "Don't expect me on the cross-country team," I told Tiffany. "I've got better things to do with my afternoons. And my energy."

"But I thought for sure you would." She appeared genuinely surprised, even a little disappointed.

"Brad sent me a postcard today," I announced, changing the subject.

"What did he say?"

"Two simple words—*send pizza*." I grinned.

Tiffany leaped from the fence and shoved me. "We'll do it!" she gushed. "Tonight!" She didn't give me a chance to say no as she suddenly walked backward to her car, pointing at me and jabbering, "I think Dad will let me take the car. Check with your parents. See if you can go. I'll shower and be back in fifteen minutes."

"You can't get ready in fifteen minutes," I objected.

"I'll do it in thirty."

"Do you know how far it is to Ephraim? And Brad's probably got a curfew. We probably can't even see him."

She jabbed a finger in my direction. "Don't stand around talking. We're wasting time!"

Forty minutes later I was in the Bronco, riding out of Eden. It hadn't been easy talking Mom and Dad into our excursion. Mom had only caved when I promised that I'd take Brad some of her bottled fruit and a loaf of homemade bread. We also promised to be back shortly after midnight.

"You know this is crazy," I said, adjusting the seatbelt. "We don't even know where his dorm is."

"Ephraim's tiny. There's probably only one dorm in the whole town. We'll find it."

It was nine thirty when we pulled into Ephraim. We had picked up an extra-large ham pizza and a two-liter bottle of orange soda in Provo because we weren't sure there would be anything open in Ephraim. We finally found Brad's dorm and sent up a message to his room. He emerged barefoot, wearing shorts and a neon-pink tank top.

"I don't believe it," he laughed, looking us up and down and glancing at his watch.

I flipped open the pizza box. "It's cold, but it's still pizza."

"I guess you know if the coach catches me out here with you two, he'll kick me off the team," he said with his mouth full as the three of us found a secluded place on the lawn in the shadows and sat down. "But a ham pizza is worth it," he added, still chewing. He looked around. "Don't tell me you forgot the orange soda."

I jumped up, ran to the car, and brought the bottle of soda. "We don't have cups."

He studied the two of us. "Do either of you have a communicable disease, one that I don't already have?" He didn't wait for an answer. "Then it doesn't matter if we share the same bottle." He took a long drink and wiped his mouth with the back of his hand. "Just don't backwash." Studying the bottle, he shrugged and then handed it to Tiffany. "No big deal. It's too dark to see the floaties anyway. But just don't leave any big chunks floating in there."

"How do things look on the team?" I asked as he started his second slice of pizza.

Brad chewed without answering. Finally swallowing, he set his slice down on a napkin. "I keep telling myself not to get my hopes up, but I think the coach is leaning my way. Anderson's been with the program longer, but things haven't clicked for him." He stared out into the parking lot. "Actually it's kind of scary because things have clicked great for me. I mean, it's like the pieces of this great big puzzle have just fallen into place. Everything's been right on. I think I'll start when we play Eastern Arizona down there two weeks from tomorrow."

"How far is it to Eastern Arizona?" I asked hopefully.

"I think you can make it in fourteen hours." He grinned. "What do you say, Tiffany?"

"Dad would have a slight objection to my taking the car to Arizona," she laughed.

The three of us munched pizza in silence for a moment, then Brad chuckled and gave me a quick shove. "What am I making big plans for? Anderson will probably start."

Tiffany and I stayed with Brad until close to eleven o'clock. As we stood outside the dorm door, having a hard time letting him go, he grinned and said, "Thanks for coming. I've been lonely."

"How do you get lonely in the middle of seventy football players?" Tiffany asked skeptically.

He heaved a sigh. "It's not the same, not the same as the three of us. We've got this . . ." He groped for the word. "I guess it's chemistry, a kind of magic. I miss that."

"He wants us to make another trip." Tiffany giggled. "You'll have to buy the pizza next time."

"I'm good for a pizza." He turned to me. "How's cross-country going?"

I glanced at Tiffany. She ducked her head, trying to hide her grin. "It's going," I answered with a straight face. "But fortunately it's not going with me as part of the team."

"You didn't go out?" He seemed genuinely stunned. "But I thought that was the plan."

"That was your plan, not mine."

Brad studied me. "You know, Chris, I think you're a chicken," he declared.

"Because I don't go out for cross-country?" I laughed. "Then the world's full of chickens. And you're part of the yellow-livered flock."

He shook his head. "No, it doesn't have anything to do with cross-country," he explained dispassionately. "You've got athletic potential, Chris."

"No," I disagreed, laughing. "You're the athlete in the family, not me."

"That's what I'm saying," he came back triumphantly. "You figure because I've gone out and played that you can't because you're afraid to follow me. You're probably better than I am, but you're afraid to try."

I didn't respond. Instead I folded my arms, smiled blankly, and tried not to fidget. Brad was treading on a tender nerve, but I didn't want him to suspect that. I didn't have any illusions of ever being as good as Brad; therefore, I had decided long ago that I would watch from the sidelines and let Brad take the playing field. "Do you think I can quarterback better than you, Brad?" I questioned smugly.

He shrugged. "Maybe quarterback isn't your position," he admitted. "But you're faster than me. You jump higher than I do. You'd make a great wide receiver. You and I could have been a team. But you're afraid to compete. You go hide in your books. And there's no question that you're good at the books, but you could be good in sports, too."

There was more truth to what Brad said than I wanted to admit. "Maybe you're right," I conceded. "Maybe I could have made it." I shrugged indifferently. "But it's a little late for that. I'll stick to my books. I'm not *afraid* of them."

Brad took in a long, deep breath and then exhaled in a sudden blast. "Oh, well, it was worth a try." He grinned. "I'm probably a chicken too. I know I'm never going to be a scholar like you, so I stay clear of the books. I'm content to stand on the sidelines and watch you succeed. I guess we're both chickens. But," he quickly added, raising a forefinger, "we ought to get over our yellow-livered, chicken ways. I'll hit the books, and you go out for cross-country."

I laughed and shook my head. "Nice try, Brad. I'm not interested in getting out of my chicken suit for the cross-country team."

"How are you going to get ready for our big marathon?"

"I hate to break this to you, Brad, but I'm not going to run a marathon either."

Brad shrugged and turned to Tiffany, who had quietly stood by listening to our discussion. "Well then, Tiffany, I guess you're the one that's going to play ball for Chris. I'm going to miss watching your volleyball and basketball games. This is your big year."

"You weren't ever all that great about catching my games," Tiffany chided him. "If Chris hadn't been there to cheer me on," she said, nodding in my direction, "I wouldn't have had a cheering section."

"I came when I could," he countered. "Besides, I was the one that sent Chris all the time. He knew that if I couldn't be there, he was to cheer twice as loud and make a few loud, obnoxious calls to the refs." He shrugged. "Let me know how you do this season. Who knows, maybe I'll be able to sneak up to a few of your games."

"I won't count on it. I'll just keep depending on Chris to cheer me on."

I laughed and held out my hand. "Catch you later, Brad." He took my hand, shook it, and then embraced me. "You're going to get that starting spot," I told him. "I can feel it."

CHAPTER FOUR

The following Friday, as I shuffled into the house after school, the phone rang. Nobody else seemed to be home, so I was tempted to ignore it, assuming it wouldn't be for me. After the eighth or ninth ring, though, I picked up the receiver.

"Why don't you answer the phone?" Brad barked playfully before I even said hello.

"Brad," I stammered in surprise.

"Tonight's when you should bring pizza." He burst out laughing. "Celebration time!"

"You're going to start?"

"No," he came back dryly. "I called to tell you I'll be sitting the bench next Saturday at Eastern Arizona." He laughed, his excitement contagious. "Coach says he's got a gut feeling it'll work out. Anderson's a bit bummed over the whole thing," he added softly, sadly.

"The coach has to go with the best guy," I argued enthusiastically. "Mom and Dad will be pumped. We'll make the Scottsdale game in Ephraim for sure."

Everybody at home was excited about Brad's good fortune, and that's all we talked about for the next few days. Dad even toyed with the idea of driving to Arizona. All through Brad's years of playing ball, Dad had been a faithful follower, rarely missing one of Brad's athletic contests. It was difficult for him to stay in Eden when Brad was going to be starting his first game as a college quarterback, but Brad convinced him not to make the trip. "Look, Dad," he explained, "I might go down there and blow it after a few plays—then you'd watch me warm the bench for the rest of the game. And then you'd still have a fourteen-hour drive back to Eden. Not a great way to spend a week-end. No, let me do this one alone. You'll see me when we play Scotts-dale Community."

The Thursday before Brad's first game, I stayed after school to do a short research project for English, and I didn't get home till late afternoon. The house was empty. I fed Dad's Angus cattle, did some other outside chores, and then went to my room to study for a Government quiz. Around seven o'clock I realized that I was still alone in the house. That's when the phone rang. It was Mom, and she began to ramble. She was in Provo at the hospital. Brad was all right, but he would have to have surgery. The doctors were optimistic, though. She wanted me to pick up Lisa at Tricia Wilson's house and call the Sandersons and tell Randy to return home and . . .

"Mom," I cut in, struggling to unscramble my brain, "what's going on?"

She took a breath and paused. "Brad broke his arm in practice today," she said slowly and quietly. I could picture her clutching the phone, her face pale and tense with worry.

"His throwing arm?" I rasped.

"No, but it's a bad break. He's scheduled for surgery tomorrow."

"But his first game's in two days," I blurted out. "Why were they playing so rough? Doesn't the coach know anything?"

"It was a freak accident. Brad tripped and fell. Two linemen got tangled up and stumbled over him, and one landed on him."

I stood, shaking, with the receiver to my ear. "How long's he out?" I whispered.

"They won't even cast it for a week after his surgery. He'll be in the cast till November."

"The whole season." It wasn't a question, just an aching reality.

I didn't go to school the next day. I waited by the phone for word about Brad. He came out of surgery fine, and he was going to spend a couple of days in the hospital. Tiffany stopped by the house at the end of school. After hearing the latest report, she smiled and remarked, "I know it's his turn to buy the pizza, but he can't sneak out of the hospital."

I smiled wanly. "You mean drive to Provo? Tonight?"

She shrugged. "It's Friday. I don't have a big date. No homework."

"Will your dad let you take the car again? Mom and Dad have our car in Provo. Lisa and Randy are staying with friends, so I'll be here alone. I could sneak off."

Tiffany nodded. "I'll promise Dad that we'll be back before midnight."

It wasn't hard getting in to see Brad. The tough part was sneaking the pizza and orange soda inside without being stopped by one of the nurses. We used a duffel bag and sauntered down the hall, leaving an aromatic trail of hot ham pizza.

Brad was sitting up in bed with his left arm elevated by a series of silver cables and pulleys. He was watching TV and didn't see us until we were both inside the room.

"You just wanted to bum around and catch up on your soap operas," I accused him.

A grin crinkled his dark face when he saw us. Picking up the remote, he snapped off the TV. "Actually," he came back, "I've been waiting for you two clowns. Where's my pizza?"

"Sorry, your turn to buy," Tiffany reminded him as we stepped to the side of his bed and she set the duffel bag on the bed table.

"I could be in a coma, and you'd still expect me to come up with the pizza." Brad looked around and sniffed the air. "All right, I can smell it. You two aren't chumps after all."

Tiffany put her finger to her lips and hushed him. "What are you trying to do, get us kicked out of here? This is bootleg pizza."

"I don't care if you two get kicked out." He grinned. "Just leave the pizza. You did bring orange soda, didn't you?"

I rolled my eyes. "You don't think we'd dare forget your precious orange soda, do you?"

Brad pointed to the floor and remarked, "We could toss a blanket down there and have a regular picnic, but I'm kinda hung up right now." He nodded to the pulleys and cables. "It'll have to be a picnic in bed."

"Where are Mom and Dad?" I asked, looking around furtively. "I'm not sure I want them to catch me here. They think I'm home holding down the fort."

"They're eating someplace. But don't worry. Nobody's busting any secrets out of me."

Huddled around Brad's bed, the three of us snacked on pizza and sipped orange soda. Whenever a nurse stopped in, we hid the pizza. It was like old times, except for Brad's heavily bandaged left arm. At first we didn't mention it, choosing instead to joke and tease about other things. I was the one who finally brought up Brad's accident. "I'm sorry," I said somberly, nodding at the bandaged arm. "That's a heck of a way to end your season."

He smiled and looked up at the TV. "That's funny. Anderson told me the same thing." He shook his head. "He really was sorry. I could see it on his face." Brad flashed a crooked grin and shook his head. He toyed with the remote. "A few days ago I had everything figured out. Actually, I'd kind of changed all my plans some. I had decided that I'd play two years at Snow instead of one—then I'd go on my mission." He wet his lips. "I planned to come back with a scholarship to a four-year school, maybe redshirt my first year, and then play the next two. I had it all written out on a yellow notepad. I'd plugged in the dates and everything." He looked over at me. "I intended to go over the whole plan with you, Chris. You know, get your input, see what you thought." He shrugged as well as he could with one of his arms hanging out in front of him. "It's strange how one little thing, like stubbing your toe and tripping, can change your whole life."

"I'm sorry," I mumbled, brushing crumbs off his sheet.

"Maybe I should have just gone on my mission. I've thought a lot about that today."

"Don't beat yourself up over that," I came back. "Knowing you, you would have tripped and broken your arm walking through the doors at the MTC."

He flipped the TV on and off. "But if I'd tripped there," he said ruefully, "I'd have been where I was supposed to be." He gave my arm a slow-motion, gentle punch. "I guess you'll have to bust away from your books and be the family athlete now. Weber's cross-country team needs you." He grinned. "Are you still jogging?"

I smiled sheepishly. "I really hate to admit this to you, Brad, but I am. Not as regular as when you were there, but I still go. And I'm not training for cross-country or for your stupid marathon." I smiled weakly. "You know, I don't mind those morning jogs so much any-more. It gives me time to unwind and think."

"Hey, you do too much thinking already. You need to compete." He was serious for a moment and then smiled. "If you don't stop studying so much, your brain'll bust open. That's why I'm so careful. Most textbooks ought to have a warning label on them." He sucked in a quick breath of air, nodded slowly, and turned to Tiffany. "Tiffany, I gave you the official assignment to make an athlete out of him. What's holding you back?"

Tiffany laughed. "I've tried, but he's pretty stubborn. You should know that."

Brad studied Tiffany momentarily, then turned to me. "Is it just my medication or is she better looking every time I see her?" He looked around. "It could be the poor light in here."

Tiffany glared and playfully whacked his leg. "I'm getting tired of your snide insults. You better be careful or I'll break your leg too—I don't care if you are laid up in a hospital bed." She smiled shyly in my direction, and secretly, just so she could see, I raised my eyebrows several times in rapid succession. She gave me a warning glance and turned back to Brad.

"Tiffany is getting pretty good-looking," Brad went on. He shook his head and looked at me. "She was sure ugly when we first ran into her, but we've polished her up real good."

"I'm going to break your other arm in a minute," Tiffany retorted. "You're a real sweet guy, especially after I risked my life to smuggle pizza to you."

"I'm only messing with you, Tiffany. I'm just jealous that you won't go out with me."

"And how many times have I turned you down?"

"I'm afraid to take the chance. What college guy wants to get turned down by a little high-school girl?" He grinned and winked in my direction.

"Why don't you try me?" Tiffany came back.

Brad thought a moment and then said, "Has anybody asked you to homecoming?"

"It's a little early for that," she replied as she blushed bright red.

"Then consider yourself asked. I'll still be packing a cast, but I'll be able to dance."

Tiffany looked down and gently brushed her hand across the sheet along the edge of the bed. "Don't go making plans with me,

Brad Huish. As soon as the anesthesia wears off and you get out of here, you'll have plenty of college girls to keep you busy." She looked up. "But when homecoming rolls around, and if you don't have some other girl hanging on you, give me a call. I'll keep the night open for you. But ask me when you're not stuck in a hospital bed."

"You just keep that date open for me, Tiffany."

The nurses finally ran Tiffany and me out of Brad's room, which was lucky for me because apparently Mom and Dad showed up a few minutes later. They'd had enough surprises and stress without discovering Tiffany and me in Brad's room when they thought we were in Eden.

Brad returned home for a few days to recuperate, but then he was back at Snow. He'd decided that he could recover as easily there and not fall behind in his classes. It was like old times again as the three of us laughed and talked. But once again, after Brad was gone, Tiffany and I didn't spend as much time together.

A few weeks later in English I overheard Tory Clark mention to one of his buddies that he had asked Tiffany to homecoming. She had declined because she said she was going with Brad. Rory Weams asked her too, and he got the same answer.

A week later I ran into Tiffany as she was heading out to her car after school. She offered me a ride so I wouldn't have to take the bus. "No volleyball practice today?"

She shook her head. "We've got a game tomorrow. Coach is letting us go tonight."

We got in her car and started home. As we drove up the mountain, I noticed how summer was evolving into fall. The car window was rolled up most of the way because the air was crisp over the mountain pass, especially in the shadows. Eden had already had its first frost, and more cold threatened. The leaves were rapidly changing, splashing the hillsides with traces of red and yellow against a background of green. A full explosion of dazzling colors was only days away.

"I got a card from Brad yesterday," Tiffany announced, taking my attention away from the mountain.

"What did the big college man have to say?"

She laughed. "He's having a great time. He said he's almost glad he broke his arm because it gives him more time to goof around. He's just kidding though."

"Did he mention homecoming? It's in two weeks."

She laughed and looked away. "I'm sure he's already forgotten that. He was just messing around that night and under anesthesia."

"So who are you going with?"

She laughed. "I'll sit homecoming out this year."

"I hear you got nominated for homecoming queen."

"Anybody can get nominated," she came back, blushing.

"I'm running a pretty vigorous campaign for you," I kidded her. "I figure I can round up the votes to at least make you an attendant. I might have to threaten a few freshmen, pay off some sophomores, but I'll pull something off."

"Spare me," she groaned, adjusting the rearview mirror. "The last thing I need is to be a homecoming anything." She tapped on the steering wheel with her fingers. "Are you going?"

I laughed. "I've got about as much interest in the homecoming dance as I have in going out for cross-country." I shook a finger at her. "And don't let Brad tell you to get on my case about being more social. I'll bag the dance and catch a movie instead."

"I'll go with you."

"Don't kid yourself. By the time you've been voted homecoming queen, you'll have a ton of guys asking you out. I'll just catch the movie by myself."

"I've already made up my mind that I'm not going to homecoming unless . . ." She hesitated and giggled.

"Unless what?" I pressed.

"Nothing," she came back, biting down on her lower lip to fight off a smile.

"Unless Brad takes you," I finished for her.

"Maybe."

I heaved a sigh. "So you're still in love?"

"It's just a little crush now." She laughed. "But it would be kind of fun to glide into the homecoming dance holding on to Brad Huish's arm and see all the girls' envious looks."

A few days later Brad called home. We joked for a while, and then I asked how his classes were going.

"I'm buried. College isn't like high school. I don't know what I'd do if I were still playing ball. I'm getting decent grades, though. Not your kind of grades, but good for me."

"How's your social life?" There was a long pause. "Brad, that was a question."

"Oh, I get out some."

"You probably get out a lot. That's probably why you're buried."

He laughed. "I'm not making any confessions to you. You're not my mother." He laughed again. "I'll admit I'm having a pretty good time, though."

"Anybody in particular?"

"Did Mom write these questions down for you?" he asked suspiciously. "Or is she just listening in on the other phone?"

"I'm just trying to vicariously live your college life." I hesitated and then remarked casually, "Homecoming's next Friday."

"You going? It's your senior year. You'd better go. If you stay home and study, I'll drive up there and pound on you. Get a date."

"What about you? Are you coming to homecoming?"

"I have midterms next week. And there's a dance down here Friday. I've got a date."

"I thought you were taking Tiffany to homecoming."

"What?"

"You asked Tiffany to homecoming. Remember in the hospital? You told her to reserve homecoming for you."

Brad was quiet for a moment. "But we were just messing around. We weren't serious."

"Maybe you weren't serious, but she's been planning on it."

"Tiffany? She doesn't want to go with me. There are lots of guys that want to ask her."

I didn't say anything for a moment as a shadow of irritation stirred inside me. "Maybe she wants to go with you." There was an edge to my voice.

"Chris, I can't go with her. I'm booked this week."

"You double-booked then. You asked Tiffany first. You better at least call her and tell her you're standing her up, because she's planning on going with you. She's been planning on it ever since we visited you in the hospital."

"I'm not standing her up, Chris," he responded defensively. "We never had a date, not a real one. But I'll give her a call. Right now. She'll understand."

Later that evening, Tiffany stopped by—the first time she'd been by the house since Brad went back to school. "I got bored with studying," she announced. "I need some distraction. Do you want to go for a walk? It's chilly, so you'll need a coat."

Wearing jackets, we started down the road toward the Maverik store, which was about a half-mile walk. October was cool enough in the valley that we could see our breath. Tiffany was pleasant and talkative. I just mainly listened as she grumbled about a chemistry project, laughed about her volleyball practice, and speculated about Weber High's latest romantic rumors.

When we reached the Maverik store, I bought us each a bottle of juice, and we split a Hostess pie.

"Brad called this evening," Tiffany reported as we left the store and stepped back into the cool evening. "Did you tell him he was supposed to take me to homecoming?"

Her question caught me off guard. "Well, he did ask you," I answered defensively.

She laughed. "Chris, it was all a big joke." She took a bite of pie and chewed. Licking her fingers, she went on. "When you're at college, the last thing you want to do is go back to high school and hang out with the gang." She paused, and I knew she was making excuses for him. My cheeks colored. Tiffany touched my arm and laughed. "Besides, what would I do at the homecoming dance?" She breathed deeply and exhaled slowly. I could see a puff of her breath in the moonlight. She laughed. "Formal dances have never been my thing. I'm more comfortable getting all sweaty hitting a volleyball or bouncing a basketball."

I glanced at Tiffany. She dated pretty regularly. In fact, lately she'd been asked out quite a bit, so I suspected that she was merely covering up for her disappointment in not going with Brad. "I'm fine about not going to homecoming," she said good-naturedly. "So don't be sending Brad on a guilt trip. Besides, I'm going with you to the movies."

Tuesday evening while I was in the barn spreading straw in the stalls, Tiffany slipped into the barn dressed in her volleyball practice gear. I nodded to a pitchfork leaning against the wall. "Grab a fork and make yourself useful."

I was only kidding, but she grabbed the fork and started pitching straw. "You're working late," she commented.

"All in a day's work," I replied.

I glanced at Tiffany as she worked. Her kneepads were pulled down to her ankles, her hair coming unbraided and hanging down about her face. She looked tired. "Don't step in anything suspicious," I warned. "If it's soft and gushy, it probably stinks, too."

"I'll be careful," she returned plaintively.

"I was kidding about you helping out. I'm almost finished." I grinned. "You'll make me feel like a jerk if you start doing my chores."

She laughed. "But I want to make you feel guilty."

We worked in silence for a while, and then she asked quietly, "Chris, can I ask a huge favor? But you have to promise not to laugh," she warned quickly, pointing a finger at me.

"Don't tell me you flunked Howard's pop quiz and need me to tutor you for his exam."

She smiled sheepishly. "Would you believe I pulled an eighty-nine percent, the high score in my class? I think Mr. Howard thought I cheated, even though I guessed through the whole thing. Mr. Howard would really be annoyed if he knew someone actually guessed and still passed one of his famous quizzes." She kicked at a pile of straw. "Anyway, I need to ask you a different favor."

"How much will it cost me?" I joked, leaning on my fork. She smiled shyly but wouldn't look at me. "I'm listening," I continued. "Let me have it."

She hesitated, debating how to word the question while she continued spreading the straw using her feet and the fork. "I'm one of the homecoming-queen attendants," she said suddenly. "Isn't that weird?" She stopped, stood in the middle of the stall, and looked herself up and down. "Do I look like homecoming royalty?" She shook her head and laughed.

"Well, maybe if you weren't all sweaty and standing in manure up to your ankles you could pass for something. Royalty might be a stretch." I grinned and tossed the pitchfork so that it stuck in a bale of straw.

"Your confidence is so comforting." She leaned her pitchfork against the wall.

"Congratulations," I said, smiling proudly. "I told you that I was running a strong campaign for you—stuffing ballot boxes, paying a few sophomores to vote for you, and threatening the freshmen with bodily harm if they didn't vote for you. But I was kinda hoping you'd be the queen. It just proves that a little voter corruption can't always make you queen."

"Very funny." She dropped onto a bale of straw. "I'm not queen material, even if I weren't all sweaty and tromping around in manure. I can play ball and run and . . ."

"And be everybody's friend," I filled in for her. "As far as I'm concerned, that's what's most important."

She smiled weakly. "Thanks, but I still feel really stupid. This royalty stuff is supposed to be for the cheerleaders." She seemed helpless, even vulnerable. As much as I enjoyed teasing and tormenting her, suddenly I wanted to protect her. "Will you take me to the dance? That's my huge favor." She forced a smile. "I just have to be there for the coronation," she quickly added, brightening a little. "And I only have to dance once—while they play the theme song. You wouldn't even have to dance that one dance because I'll be dancing with one of the king's attendants. There are probably a million other things you'd rather do Friday night, and I—"

"I'd love to go," I cut her off, grinning. "I've never gone anyplace with royalty." I looked down at my feet. "I guess that means I'll have to kick the manure off my own boots and put on a clean pair of Levi's. I even have one without a patch. Of course, both knees are worn through and the legs are frayed at the bottom. And Mom will probably even make me take a bath."

While I joked, she pushed up from the bale of straw, stepped over, and hugged me. She touched my cheek with the back of her hand as she stepped back. "I knew I could count on you, Chris. You're always there. That's what I love about you."

"I thought you loved Brad," I teased, shaking an accusing finger at her.

"I do. From a distance. Remember?" She started backing toward the barn door. "I won't take up a big chunk of your night. We can still go to the movies if you want."

"If I go," I called after her, "it's a full-fledged date. All the whistles and bells."

She shook her head. "You don't have to do that. This shouldn't cost much. I'll even get you a hamburger on the way home."

"Then it's no deal." I was serious. "It's got to be a full-fledged date." I stared at her and added a gentle warning, "Otherwise, you have to get somebody else to take you." I shrugged, trying to justify myself. "I've never been to a formal dance. It will impress Brad. He'll think I'm finally coming out of my social shell. He told me that if I didn't go to homecoming, he'd drive up here and pound me. So really, are you trying to get me beat up?"

Tiffany stopped smiling. Slowly she walked back to me. For several seconds she studied me, traces of tears in her eyes, then she reached out and hugged me again. This time she really squeezed and didn't let me go for a long time. When she finally released me, she whispered, "Thanks, Chris. You're a great friend, the best." Then she disappeared out the back door.

* * *

The night I picked Tiffany up for homecoming I was a bit nervous. I don't know how many hundreds of times I had been to her house and vice versa, but this was different. I was picking Tiffany up for a date, a formal one. I wasn't exactly panicking, but I did have my share of butterflies.

Tiffany wore a burgundy formal and looked beautiful. As soon as I saw her, I was certain that if the guys at Weber High had seen her this way, they would have easily voted her queen. I was also sure that Brad would kick himself if he ever found out he had passed up a chance to go with Tiffany looking like this.

I was glad I had decided to make this date more than a duty job. I hadn't had a lot of time to plan, but I bought her the best corsage I could find. We went to dinner at the Blue Door and ordered steak and lobster. At the dance, when the royalty was announced, Sid Downing, one of the king's attendants and a popular football jock, escorted Tiffany into the spotlight. When the theme song played, as was customary, the three royalty couples began to dance while everyone else stood and watched. The music hadn't played thirty seconds, however, when Tiffany spotted me standing next to Sid's date, and with an impulsive flair, pulled Sid over to us and left him with his date and took me out on the floor to finish the dance.

"This is just for the royalty," I mumbled, embarrassed. "I shouldn't be out here."

She smiled. "What are they going to do, take away my attendant's crown?" She laughed. "I didn't want to be an attendant in the first place," she whispered teasingly and lightly pinched the back of my neck.

When I took Tiffany home and walked her to the front door, she stood there for a moment shivering. "If I had known a formal dance could be this much fun, I would have asked you sooner." She giggled.

"But you were wishing I was Brad," I teased her. "And none of the other girls were standing around with wildly envious looks when they saw us dancing." I held up my hands and shook my head. "I can understand. You'll always be in love with Brad." I grinned. "You might end up marrying him, but I'll still be the one who took you to the homecoming dance."

Biting down gently on her lower lip, she looked up at me. "Thanks for being who you are, Chris," she said seriously. She gave me a quick, unexpected hug and then slipped into the house.

CHAPTER FIVE

Brad's cast came off the first week in November and he started physical therapy immediately. He did have one minor setback, however. His doctor told him that he would need some simple reconstructive surgery the first of January. But Brad was undaunted, maintaining a bright outlook and continuing his studies at Snow.

As Christmas vacation approached, our family was excited to have Brad home for three weeks. I sensed Tiffany's excitement too. "If we get snowshoes and bundle up really well," she told me just before Brad's return, "we can take him up the mountain for another steak fry."

"What do you say we crank up the heat, pop popcorn, and watch a movie in the living room?"

"You're no fun," she pouted playfully. "He'll want to do something thrilling and daring."

The day Brad returned to Eden I rushed home after school. I didn't need to, though, because he didn't appear till after six o'clock. When he did arrive, the whole family met him at the door as he lugged his suitcase and duffel bag inside. There were hugs, back slapping, joking, and teasing as he stood with his coat still on and his bags on the floor. Although I had seen him off and on since he'd left Eden in August, he seemed older, more mature. I thought back to his remark about things never being the same again, that all of us would change. I was surprised, and a little sad, that it was happening so soon.

"You look great!" my brother Randy burst out. "Do you think you'll be able to play ball next fall?" He looked Brad up and down in an appraising manner. With straight brown hair, blue eyes, and a strong, agile body, Randy was a smaller version of Brad. He didn't have Brad's handsome looks, but he seemed to have all of his brother's athletic prowess. In fact, as Brad had watched him participate in sports, he had predicted that eventually Randy would be the family's best athlete. That vote of confidence from Brad made Randy proud, and he tried hard to live up to his hero's expectations. "I'll bet you'll make the team next year," Randy proclaimed with a wide, toothy grin.

"Brad will be on his mission next fall," I reminded Randy.

Brad glanced at me and then back at Randy. "Before I do any planning, I better wait until after my surgery in January," Brad said, smiling. "If the doctor slips and chops off my arm, I won't be much good for anything." He laughed and tousled Randy's hair. "Mom wrote that you made eighteen points in your last basketball game, half your team's total."

Randy grinned appreciatively. "The ball was just hot."

"You're not going to trade football in for basketball, are you?" Brad asked somewhat accusingly. "Weber is going to need another Huish for quarterback."

Randy shook his head. "But I've decided not to play quarterback. I think I'll be a better running back."

Brad smiled and nodded, looking him up and down. "You're built like a running back too, and you'll be bigger than either Chris or me. And I think you'll have more speed."

While Brad praised Randy and gave him suggestions on his basketball, Dad stood by and beamed, occasionally making a comment. Lisa stood next to Brad and kept her arms wrapped around his waist, content to be close to him. After a while, though, Brad tugged her arms from around him, held her out at arm's length, and asked seriously, "And what has my little sister been doing while Randy's been out playing ball?" Before she could answer, he pushed on skeptically, "You haven't been practicing cheers, have you? We're not having any cheerleaders in this house."

Lisa scrunched up her freckle-covered nose and stuck out her tongue. "I like being a cheerleader," she spouted back.

"Being a cheerleader is a waste of good talent," Brad grumbled, shaking his head. "Cheerleaders just stand on the sidelines and watch. You want to be out on the floor playing—that's where the action is. You're too athletic to be doing high kicks and splits. With a little practice you could be competing for Randy's running-back spot." He reached out and tugged playfully on one of her braids as Randy took a swipe at him.

Lisa whirled and jerked away. "Somebody's got to cheer," she challenged.

"Not you," Brad came back. "Look at Tiffany. She doesn't cheer. She plays."

After a few more minutes of silly banter, Brad glanced at his watch and announced, "Hey, I'll have to catch up on everything later. I've got an appointment in thirty minutes. I better have a quick shower."

"You haven't even taken your coat off," Mom protested, frowning and coming from the kitchen where she'd retreated after giving Brad a hug and a kiss. "Dinner's almost ready."

"Save me some." Brad cringed and ducked as if she was going to hit him. "I'm dying for your home cooking."

I followed Brad upstairs. He tossed his bags on his bottom bunk and kicked off his shoes. "Who's your appointment with?" I questioned suspiciously.

He pulled his shirt over his head and tossed it on his pillow. "Actually, it's more like a date," he whispered sheepishly, glancing toward the door as though afraid someone might overhear him. "Appointment sounds better when I'm skipping out on Mom's dinner."

"She fixed it just for you."

"Then don't tell her. I'm driving to Tremonton to see Stacy Miller, a girl I've been hanging out with. I'm going to meet her parents."

I shook my head. "You've been with her all semester. What about spending time with your family?" I chided him.

Brad grinned. "We'll have the whole holiday together."

"Unless you decide to spend most of it with Stacy."

Brad laughed. "Not a chance." He then cleared his throat, suddenly becoming serious. "You remember what Randy said downstairs a few minutes ago, about me being ready for football next fall?" I didn't say anything, and Brad didn't wait for me. "I've started thinking again." He studied me, but I kept my expression blank. I knew what was coming, and it was hard not to feel the stinging bite of disappointment. "I really didn't get my chance to play," he went on, starting to pace the floor and stare at his feet. "It was almost there, and then it slipped away. I'm so close, Chris. I don't know if I can just let it slip away forever."

"So the mission goes on the back burner again," I stated flatly.

"Only for a few months. At the end of the season, I'll leave on my mission. Probably in December or January."

"So we won't leave together?" I couldn't help sounding hurt; I'd grown fond of the idea.

"We'll be out there together. I'll just head out a little after you."

I shrugged and turned away. "Sounds like you've got it all worked out."

"I'm running it past you, Chris. What do you think?"

"You don't need my okay," I answered dully.

"I don't *need* it, Chris. I *want* it. I want you to feel good about it. I want you to support me."

I faced him and chuckled. "Brad, you don't have to ask me. I'm just your kid brother."

"But we've planned things together. I told you I'd go with you, that we'd go together." He shook his head. "But I want to play one good season of ball, Chris. I've got a fire in my gut when it comes to that. I know you don't understand because ball isn't your big thing, but it's one of mine. And I want the mission, too. This way I feel I can have them both." He was practically pleading with me. "What do you say, Chris?"

At that moment I suddenly hurt for Brad. I knew that this decision wasn't easy for him. He was in turmoil. Something told me, though, that if I told Brad that he shouldn't play next fall, that he should go on his mission, he would have done it. I realized then how much my older brother valued my opinion. I also didn't feel like I should be making that decision for him. "I guess you better plan to play ball," I answered hoarsely, and cleared my throat. "But if you do, you better play better than you've ever played in your life." I smiled. "And when I'm off in Mongolia or some other place, you'd better write me a long letter every week telling me how the game went."

Brad grinned. "I'm not much of a writer, but I can do that. And we might still be companions. I might get sent to Mongolia, and you'll be my senior companion."

"Yep. It's about my turn to boss you around."

I was in bed when Brad returned home after midnight, but I was still awake. Brad undressed in the dark, stirred around in the room, hummed faintly, and eventually slipped into the bed below mine. He lay there for a moment and then whispered, "Hey, Chris, you still awake?"

I took in a long breath and answered, "How was your appointment?"

Brad chuckled. "It was a really good appointment." There was a long silence. "Chris," he said slowly, "you're all right."

I laughed softly. "What brought that on? Do you need a loan or something?"

He snickered. "Maybe later." He was quiet for another moment. "You know, when you visited me in the hospital," he mused, "I was feeling like I'd lost everything. I'd counted on that starting quarter-back position. And it wasn't like I'd lost it to Anderson with a chance to win it back. I was washed up and couldn't do a thing about it. It was like all the doors of opportunity had slammed in my face at the same time. As Dad used to say, 'I was feelin' lower than a snake's belly.' I actually physically ached. I'd never felt like that."

He paused, then chuckled. "Then you came. And you made me believe that I still had a chance to put the few broken pieces of my life back together. You were like a breath of fresh air in the bottom of a stinkin' black pit." He coughed and shifted his weight on the bottom bunk, making it squeak and creak. "You're a great guy, Chris, an awesome brother." Once again he paused. "Do you know what I kept thinking tonight?" He didn't wait for me to answer. "I kept wishing that you and Tiffany were with me, that the three of us were hanging out together."

"Were Stacy and her parents that boring?"

Brad laughed. "Actually, I got to thinking of you and Tiffany on my way home."

"Now the truth busts out. As long as you were with Stacy, every-thing was fine and peachy, but then on the lonely ride home you—"

"It's not like that," Brad countered, trying not to laugh.

"Don't feel guilty. You can't drag Tiffany and me around with you all your life. Besides, aren't you the one who told me that everything was going to change, everything was going to be different?"

"Some things don't change, Chris. Like you. Thanks for being a great guy."

"Hey, Brad, believe me, things are changing. You used to love being at home. Now you can't wait to ditch your family so you can go to one of your *appointments*."

Brad chuckled. "All right, stop rubbing it in. If you saw Stacy, you'd want to be with her too. I'd let you see her, but she'd probably decide she liked you better than me."

"Yeah, I'm sure that's going to happen."

"We ought to double, though."

"I don't do appointments, Brad."

"You could get a date. You could even go with Tiffany. She'd go with you."

I chuckled, thinking about Tiffany. "Something tells me that Tiffany wouldn't be crazy about that arrangement."

* * *

Although I wasn't sure it would happen, Tiffany, Brad, and I did get together during the holidays. It was almost like old times, except most evenings Brad headed off for Tremonton to be with Stacy Miller. It seemed he was getting serious, and just before the end of the holiday, after the three of us had spent a day building snowmen in the pasture and having a rollicking snowball fight, Brad left to get ready for a date. Tiffany and I tromped back to the house, wet and shivering.

"Do you think he'll marry her?" Tiffany asked as the snow crunched under our boots.

"You mean Stacy? How can he? Isn't he going to marry you?"

"Very funny," she responded dryly, snatching a handful of snow and throwing it at me.

"You're not giving up hope, are you? Competition is good. It makes you stronger."

She drove into me with her shoulder, knocking me over. "You just love to harass me."

I staggered to my feet and pushed her away when she lunged at me again. "You can't let somebody like Stacy horn in on your territory," I told her, laughing.

She tugged on her gloves and then started brushing snow from the arms of her coat. "I gave up on marrying Brad a long time ago."

She smiled wanly. "That doesn't mean that I can't still have a crush on him. At least until someone else actually marries him. Then I'll back off." She laughed. "Remember if you breathe a word of this to anybody, I'll break both your legs."

"Maybe if Brad knew you were in love with him," I kidded her, "he'd drop Stacy flat."

"Just make sure you don't go and tell him. Do you hear?"

I smiled and nodded my head.

* * *

Brad had his minor surgery in Provo the middle of January. It was outpatient surgery, so Stacy drove him back to Ephraim the same day. A couple of weeks later he came home on a Saturday afternoon to spend the weekend with us. He was using his injured arm almost as though nothing had happened. "I've started packing my football around with me everywhere," he told me as we worked in the barn changing the oil in the truck. He laughed. "I even take it to class. I've been lifting and I started running back in October when I had my cast on. I thought I'd be way out of shape, but things aren't half as bad as I thought they'd be. And things are clicking again. I can't believe how good I feel, and I can hardly wait for spring drills to start."

"Next fall's your big chance," I said, pouring oil into the engine. "But when I'm in Mongolia, if I get a letter telling me that you're just sitting the bench, so help me, I'll come back here and romp all over you."

He chuckled. "I promise you that I'll never send you a letter like that." He shrugged and added, "I might have to lie a little in my letters, but I'll never tell you I'm sitting on the bench." He flashed me a grin. "I'm hoping it's a good year." He hesitated, leaning thoughtfully against the fender. "But anything can happen, Chris." He pressed his lips together and then blurted out, "You could wait to send your papers in and go next January with me. That way you'd be able to see me play."

I didn't respond immediately, and a rather long, awkward silence ensued. "Look, Brad," I finally said, "I'd like to see you play. I really would. But you don't need me here so you can play ball. You can write and tell me about it."

There was another pause. "I talked to my bishop in Ephraim about a mission," he said quietly.

"At the end of the season?"

"Maybe sooner." He glanced over at me.

I finished pouring oil in the engine. "And football?" I didn't give him time to answer. "I thought you'd decided to play, then go. Wasn't that the plan?" I grumbled sharply. I tossed the empty oil container on the ground. "What did the bishop say?"

"That it was up to me."

I wiped my hands on an oily rag. Reaching up, I pulled the hood down. It closed with a loud, echoing bang.

"What are you going to do, Chris? I mean, after you graduate."

I shrugged, tossed the rag down, and leaned against the truck's grill. "Work during the summer to earn some money, then go on my mission."

"Do you think I should have done that?"

I smiled. "How many colleges do you think are asking me to play football for them? Or run cross-country? Or do basket weaving?" I folded my arms and shook my head. "We're different, Brad."

"What if you were a big-shot football star, Chris? You'd still go on your mission, wouldn't you?"

"I guess I'll never have to worry about that one."

Brad heaved a sigh. "I've wondered about filling out my papers—you know, having them all ready so that all I have to do is turn them in to the bishop. I'll still go through spring drills. If things go well in football, I'll hold my papers till later. If spring drills are a bomb and it doesn't look like I'll be playing much next fall, I'll turn the papers in and leave on my mission sometime during the summer. That way we'll still go together, like we'd planned." He paused. "What do you think?" He pushed away from the truck. "Don't even answer that. You'd just go on your mission." He started picking up the tools and cans around the truck. "I wish I was like you," he added softly.

"Like me?" I laughed. "Nobody wants to be like me."

Brad looked at me and smiled ruefully. "Maybe I do."

Another awkward silence followed. Finally I kicked at one of the truck tires. "Are you still doing a little dating?" I asked, changing the subject.

He chuckled. "You won't believe this, but I'm actually hitting the books pretty hard and carrying sixteen credit hours. Shoot! I'm a regular scholar. I spent last night—a Friday night no less—in the library. That was a first."

"Were you alone in the library?" I asked, biting back a smile.

"Now what kind of a crack is that? It wasn't like the place was deserted. There were a few other people there."

"So your Friday night date was studying in the library," I said knowingly. "That gives research a romantic twist."

"I didn't say I was in the library with her."

"Her?" I teased. "*Her* must mean Stacy. Or did you find somebody else?"

"Okay, we went to the library together. Isn't that better than going to the movies?"

"I don't know. Depends on the movie or what happened in the library. Was the library better?"

Brad picked at a splotch of mud on the truck's fender. "Why is it that I get the impression that I'm being interrogated?" he asked lightly. "By my punk brother, no less. You hardly ever go on a date, and you've got to harass me about studying in the library with a girl."

"I wasn't harassing you," I laughed. "I was just asking about your week. You're the one that's getting all defensive. I don't care if you've got a steady girlfriend and—"

"I didn't say that I had a steady girlfriend. Stacy and I are just . . ."

"Brad," I said, pretending to exude great patience, "when you're with a girl all the time, that's pretty steady, wouldn't you say?"

"We're friends. And get that annoying smirk off your face."

I nodded knowingly. "That's a new twist. You're not going steady because she's just a casual friend. But you're with this casual friend all the time. But you're just casual about the whole thing. In other words you're casually going steady with one of your casual friends."

"I can see this conversation is going downhill fast."

I laughed. "I'm just trying to understand you, Brad."

"I've got a ton of homework to do," he returned, trying hard not to laugh and starting to move toward the barn door, "and it doesn't leave me time to answer dumb, probing questions from my kid brother."

CHAPTER SIX

One evening, the first part of February, I was rewriting a paper for English when Lisa knocked on my open bedroom door. I glanced in her direction. She stood there with a plate of chocolate brownies covered in green mint frosting and sprinkled with miniature chocolate chips. "They're fresh," she announced, bringing them into the room and setting them on the desk next to my computer monitor. She bent over and smelled them and then handed me a card she had been holding underneath the plate. "Tiffany dropped them off and told me to give them to you." She licked her lips. "Are you sharing?"

The brownies were arranged in a neat, circular pyramid. Reaching out, I took the one on the very top. In three large, hungry bites I devoured the whole thing while Lisa watched me, her mouth watering. Grabbing another brownie, I explained, "I'll let you have one in a second, but first I better make sure they're edible." I winked at her. "I don't want you to get sick or anything. In one huge bite, half of the second brownie disappeared.

"Has anyone told you you're a big, stingy pig?" Lisa asked matter-of-factly.

"Nobody," I mumbled with my mouth full. "You're not dropping any hints, are you?" I took another giant bite. "These really are good," I said, smacking my lips to torment Lisa. "Do you want one?"

"No," she muttered. "I just like to stand here and watch you make a pig of yourself."

"Well, Lisa, if you get tired of watching me," I went on, "you can have one." As she reached for one, I held up my index finger. "Just one. You know, I don't want you to make a pig of yourself and get sick or anything." She punched me as I went for my third brownie. "Nobody makes brownies like Tiffany," I said, closing my eyes, savoring the chocolate, minty flavor. "It's been a long time since she's sent any over."

Lisa nibbled on her brownie and picked up the card. "Aren't you going to read this?"

I grinned. "I better eat the brownies while they're fresh. Brownies can get old and stale. Cards don't. But if you want, you can read it while I eat. Tiffany's probably just telling me what a hot item I am."

Lisa rolled her eyes and tore open the envelope. As I halfheartedly returned to the computer with a half-eaten brownie in my hand, Lisa slowly read the card to herself. "What's the Sweetheart Dance?" she asked curiously, studying the plate of brownies. I stopped both eating and working. Lisa finished her brownie, licked her fingers, and remarked, "Maybe you better read this card before you have too many brownies." With her concentration back on the plate of brownies, she handed me the card that now had a speck of green mint frosting on its upper left-hand corner.

Setting the card next to my keyboard, I began to read out loud: "Dear Chris, I know I'm pretty late, but these brownies are a special thank-you for taking me to the Homecoming Dance. I don't think I ever thanked you properly. There's another reason I sent the brownies, though. In fact, it's the main reason I sent the brownies. The brownies are an invitation to the Sweetheart Dance, which is the week of Valentine's Day."

I stopped reading and looked up at Lisa, who was watching me intently, a sly smile tugging at the corners of her mouth. The Sweetheart Dance was a semiformal girl's-choice dance. My junior year Meg Mateo had asked me to go with her, but fortunately our family had already made plans to visit my grandparents in Idaho that weekend. Actually I could have easily skipped the trip to Idaho, but I was relieved to have had the excuse, so I had turned Meg down, trying to sound dutifully disappointed in the process. Meg was an okay girl, but I knew that the last thing I wanted to do was to endure a night of uncomfortable boredom while I tripped stiffly around the dance floor, straining my brain to come up with cute conversation.

I returned to Tiffany's card, continuing to read out loud: "I sent the brownies with the invitation to sweeten up the deal. I don't like to use the word *bribe*. Anyway, the deal is pretty simple. If you eat any of the brownies (a single bite or even a single chocolate chip off the top—and by the way, I've counted every single chocolate chip, so I'll know if one is missing), then you are accepting my invitation to the dance. In that case, you can finish off the whole plate of brownies. If you don't want to go to the dance, I'll stop by your place later tonight so I can pick up the whole plate of untouched brownies. Love, Tiffany. P.S. I have to admit, Chris, I know that you'll have half the brownies gone before you ever look at my card. But I guess that's your tough luck."

I put the card down, reached for another brownie, and smiled faintly. "So are you going?" Lisa asked curiously.

"She's very tricky, Lisa. She doesn't play fair at all." I bit into the brownie.

"Does that mean I get another one?"

"Go ahead," I mumbled with my mouth full. "The damage has been done." I shook my finger at her. "Lisa, when you grow up, don't grow up to be a girl. They're too devious."

"Do you want me to grow up to be a boy?" she asked with a sick grimace.

* * *

An hour later the doorbell rang. "I think it's Tiffany," Lisa called up the stairs to me.

Picking up Tiffany's plate that had four brownies remaining, I tromped down the stairs and opened the front door. Tiffany stood there, practically engulfed by her dad's huge winter parka, with a bright-red knit cap pulled down over her head and ears. She had a crooked smirk across her face. She glanced down at her plate and then remarked tauntingly, "I didn't think you'd eat so many of them before you read the card." She made a face and then burst out laughing. "I'm sorry, Chris, I just—"

"Do you want to come in?" I cut her off, stepping back from the door and motioning toward the living room. I struggled to keep a straight face. I followed Tiffany into the living room, where we both sat on the sofa. I still held the almost-empty plate of brownies.

"Do you want me to take that?" Tiffany asked, nodding toward her plate.

"Not until all of the brownies are gone," I answered dryly. "Every single crumb. I'll probably even lick the plate. I'm paying a pretty hefty price for this plate of brownies, you know." I set the plate on the coffee table. "All right, you won," I said. "You didn't win fair, but you won."

Tiffany burst out laughing as she unzipped her heavy parka. "I'm not going to make you go, Chris. It was just kind of a joke." She bit her lower lip and continued giggling.

"Oh," I countered, my face crinkling in a grin of its own. "You ask me out one minute and right after I give you your answer," I said, pointing to the nearly empty plate, "you stand me up. Now that's really good, Tiffany. That's a great way to pump up my ego."

"I didn't mean it that way."

"How do you know I didn't read the card first and then eat the brownies?"

"Because I know you." She tugged off her knit cap, and the static electricity made her hair frizz out. "I also know you're not crazy about going to dances, so I don't want to force you. But," she added softly, looking down, "there is one thing. You know Tina Mercer."

I nodded. Tina had enrolled at Weber High back in September. She was from some small town in northeastern Wyoming. She was petite, delicate, and painfully shy. The first day in Mr. Howard's government class he had asked her to introduce herself to the group. Immediately I saw the panic in her eyes. Her cheeks and neck flaming with embarrassment, she'd mumbled her name barely above a whisper, then stared down at her desk.

From the very first day, Tiffany had taken an interest in Tina. She'd pulled her into her group of friends. She'd made sure she never ate her lunch alone. She'd invited her to her volleyball and basketball games. After a few weeks, Tina had gradually crept out of her shell. She was still terribly shy and needed reassurance and encouragement, but Tiffany had made a remarkable difference in her life.

"Tina wants to go to the Sweetheart Dance. I told her that if she asked somebody, I'd double with her."

"Who's she going to ask?"

"She asked L.J. Baird."

"L.J.?" I asked, surprised. Although L.J. was a nice enough guy, he was the senior vice president and one of the more popular kids at school. "Will he go with her?"

Tiffany smiled knowingly. "He'll go," she said with a smirk, "because I told him if he even thought of turning Tina down or making her feel uneasy, then I'd just have to break both of his legs, rip his hair and eyes out by the roots, and carve my initials into the hood of his fancy red Mustang." Tiffany shrugged. "He was really pretty good about the whole thing—as soon as he knew that I meant business."

"He could probably handle losing his legs, eyes, and hair, but your initials in the hood of his Mustang probably did the trick."

"That means I need a date if I'm going to double with Tina," Tiffany went on.

"You could always just tag along as their chaperone. You wouldn't need a date then."

"I always love your suggestions, Chris," she said wryly. "However, I think I prefer the more conventional approach. I'd kind of like to have a date. And if you go, you can probably count it as a service project."

"To tell you the truth, I've met my quota of service projects for the month. I really don't need another one." I grinned.

"So is that a definite 'no' or a cowardly 'I'll think about it'?" She pursed her lips and raised one eyebrow. "Or are you just trying to make this as difficult for me as you can?"

"Since you're going to marry Brad someday, why don't you ask him?" I teased. "He needs to come home more anyway. And I doubt that he's met his monthly quota for service projects. "

Tiffany shrugged. "Brad's busy at college. Besides, he's got a girl-friend."

"Even more reason to get him back here."

"Hey, I plan to snatch him away from that Stacy girl when the time's right," she said with pretended haughty indifference. "But Brad's still at college, and you're here, so I'm asking you. Your move, tough guy."

I laughed. "Well, I guess I better go with you or you'll be carving your initials into the hood of our old Chevy truck."

"That thing's so beat up that I could carve my whole name into the hood and you'd hardly be able to tell. Believe me, your sacred truck is safe."

"I'll go with you," I told her, laughing. "After all, I did eat most of your brownies. That was the deal, and I'm not going to back out on a deal."

Tiffany suddenly became serious. "I don't want to force you, Chris. I'm really okay if you'd rather skip this dance. But I'd like to go with you more than anybody else."

"More than Brad?" I questioned, fighting back a grin.

Tiffany took a quick, deep breath. "Well, let's not push things," she laughed.

"I'll go. But I guess that means I have to wear my suit."

She pulled on her knit cap, zipped up her parka, and stood. "It's a tough life, Chris, because it does mean you have to wear a suit. A pair of greasy coveralls just won't do for this kind of dance."

* * *

Three days before the Sweetheart Dance, Tiffany called me. "Chris, I'm giving you a chance to back out," were the first words out of her mouth.

"So you're still trying to stand me up?"

"No, I'm just being up-front with you. We were going to double with Tina and L. J., but L. J. asked Tina if she would mind going with three of his buddies and their dates. She was actually okay with it. That means I can't claim this is a glorified service project," she kidded. "I kind of twisted your arm with that argument."

"The service project angle did influence me, but," I drawled, "I've kinda gotten used to the whole idea. Even wearing a suit. It's your call. If you still want to go, I'm willing. Even though it's a little tough standing in for Brad."

"Will you leave Brad out of this? I'll pick you up Friday night."

"Is there any food in this whole thing?"

There was a long pause. "Actually, I planned to cook you dinner. Can you handle a grilled steak?"

"I'll bring my appetite."

* * *

I was ready to go Friday night five or ten minutes before Tiffany drove up. With my hands stuffed in my pockets, I strolled from one room to the next, killing time. "You look handsome," Lisa remarked as she came down the stairs as I was leaving the kitchen toward the living room, carrying Tiffany's corsage. "I might even go with you," she added, "if you gave me a flower too." Then scrunching up her nose and shivering slightly, she shook her head. "But I wouldn't go with my brother."

I grinned, looking myself up and down. "You're a girl. Give it to me straight, Lisa. Will Tiffany be impressed? Will I knock her off her feet?"

She scratched her nose and studied me. "She might be impressed. I don't know about you knocking her off her feet."

"Lisa, your vote of confidence is a great comfort to me," I said sarcastically. "Thanks." She stuck out her tongue and then grinned. I faked a backhand at her. She squealed and darted back up the stairs. A moment later she called down and announced that Tiffany had just pulled into the driveway.

When the doorbell rang, I dropped stiffly onto the sofa, suddenly feeling a bit anxious, as Mom answered the door. "Well, you surely look beautiful tonight, Tiffany," Mom greeted her. "Chris is a lucky man. I think he's a bit nervous, though," she joked. "Not nervous about you, Tiffany. Just nervous to be going to a dance. Try to keep him calm."

Rubbing my hands together as I sat on the sofa, I heard the ruffled swish of fabric as Mom guided Tiffany to the living room. As soon as Tiffany stepped through the door, I caught my breath and staggered to my feet. She was beautiful in a full-length blue formal, a perfect match for her blue eyes and reddish-blond hair that she had fixed on top of her head with a few curled strands hanging down in back. Several tiny, blue artificial flowers were in her hair. She smiled shyly with her hands clasped in front of her.

She laughed and her eyes sparkled merrily. "As I was coming up the walk," she said demurely, "I realized that this is the first time I've ever stopped by here to pick someone up for a date. I've come by to invite you to go play ball, to fish, or to hike, but never to go on a date. It feels a little weird."

For a moment I just stared. Then, remembering the corsage on the sofa, I fumbled with the box, trying to get the flower out, my hands trembling and my cheeks burning. "I'm not very good with flowers," I muttered. Awkwardly, I held the corsage so Tiffany could see it. "I'd feel more comfortable handing you a basketball." I grinned and passed the flower to Mom. "Do you want to pin it on her?"

Tiffany raised an eyebrow and teased, "I was sort of hoping you'd pin it on me."

Nervously sucking in a gulp of air, I smelled the faint trace of her perfume. "If the dang thing had some Velcro, I might give it a try." I swallowed. "But I'd hate to spend the evening in the emergency room while the doctor extracted a pin from your shoulder."

Mom rescued me and helped Tiffany with the flower, then we slipped out into the chilly night. Tiffany insisted that I drive, so I helped her into her dad's car. "Where to?" I asked.

"Back to my place. Dinner's ready. It was a little hard getting dressed and fixing dinner at the same time. Mom helped some, or we'd be eating raw steak tonight."

We chatted casually until we drove up in front of Tiffany's house. Tiffany's mom and dad were waiting for us when we entered. We visited for a few minutes, then Sister Gibson wanted to take a couple of pictures. Her couple of pictures turned into a whole roll so that she could get as many different poses as possible. She might have started on a second roll of film had Tiffany not objected, "Mom, the dance will be over and you'll still be taking pictures."

"Tiffany just doesn't want so many pictures of me," I joked as Tiffany led me into their dining room, where the table was set with a white table-cloth, nice china and silverware, linen napkins, and two red candles set in crystal holders. I whistled softly. "I'm impressed," I told her.

"I hope the food tastes as good as the table looks." She blushed. "Mom set the table. I cooked the meal. Nothing fancy—steaks, baked potatoes, and green salad. I wanted to keep it simple."

I waited behind my chair while Tiffany stepped out onto the Gibsons' back patio to check the steaks that were still on the grill. I was studying the place settings when I heard a sudden screech of horror. I moved toward the glass patio doors to see what the problem was and came face to face with Tiffany, who was returning with a look of abject anguish on her face. "They're cremated!" she whimpered when she saw me. "At least they are on one side."

Tiffany's screech brought Brother and Sister Gibson charging into the dining room. "I think I might have burned the steaks a little," she explained, wincing.

"How long did you leave them there?" Brother Gibson asked.

"Well, they were about finished before I picked Chris up, so I just left them on the grill thinking they'd be fine by the time we ate—I knew Chris likes his well-done. I turned the grill down before I left, though."

Brother Gibson stepped out onto the patio. He returned a moment later with a chunk of black charcoal on the end of a long grilling fork. He turned to me and said, "Chris, good news—your steak is definitely well-done. There's absolutely no moo left. Do you like ashes?"

I couldn't help myself. I burst out laughing. "Maybe if we peel off some of the black stuff, there will be some good meat inside," I offered helpfully.

Brother Gibson shook his head. "I cut the other piece in half. If you peel off the black stuff, there's no meat at all. Believe me, this thing's cooked all the way through."

"Are they both that bad?" Sister Gibson inquired, a look of disgust on her face.

Brother Gibson nodded and held up the charred steak. "This is as good as it gets."

"Maybe with a lot of steak sauce . . ." I interjected kindly.

"There are some things that not even steak sauce can help." He turned to Tiffany. "When you turned the grill down, is it possible that you turned it up? Five more minutes and even the charcoal and ashes would have been gone."

"I'm sorry," Tiffany said, turning to me and cringing. "I didn't ever say I was a good cook." She brightened momentarily. "I do have a salad in the fridge. And the baked potatoes are in the oven." She shrugged. "At least we won't starve."

"I love baked potatoes," I responded cheerily. "Especially when I'm hungry," I added with a wide grin. "And I'm so hungry now that that piece of charcoal your dad brought in almost looks good."

"Shut up and sit down," she mumbled, flashing me a stern look that was all for show.

Brother and Sister Gibson left us to our culinary disaster, and Tiffany went into the kitchen to bring out the rest of dinner. She was gone a rather long time and when she did return, she came in with a withered brown object on the end of a dinner fork. For a moment she stood in the doorway with a crestfallen expression on her face. "I forgot to turn the oven off before I went to pick you up," she explained. "Actually, I was supposed to turn it off a few minutes before I went to pick you up. I didn't think it would matter, though. How can you burn a baked potato?" she asked rhetorically.

"I guess you found a way." I stared at the less-than-appetizing object on the end of Tiffany's fork. "I hate to break this to you, Tiffany, but I doubt that sour cream and butter will revive that potato. I think it's finally gone to that big potato field in the sky."

"We still have salad," Tiffany offered, twisting her mouth into a sad pout.

"Did you make it?" I questioned. She nodded. "I'll bet it's great," I burst out enthusiastically, clapping my hands and rubbing them together. "But," I quickly added, holding up a forefinger, "let's not find out." I cleared my throat. "Next time, why don't you set the table and let your mom fix the meal?"

Tiffany's eyes narrowed, and she glowered at me in a playful fashion. I quickly held up my hands in surrender. "That was just a suggestion." We both burst out laughing. "You know, Tiffany, if you played volleyball and basketball like you cook . . ."

"Shut up, Chris," she butted in. "I don't want to hear it."

"Can I make another suggestion?" I asked meekly, still holding up my hands. I didn't wait for her permission. "What do you say we drive down to Ogden and pick up a quick hamburger? I'll pay. I know it won't be anything like your steak dinner would have been had you . . ." I shrugged my shoulders and added in a loud whisper, "had you known what the heck you were doing . . ."

"Shut up, Chris. You're making it worse."

"That must be an emphatic yes." I grinned. "Do you think your mom will mind cleaning up the burnt offerings?"

Tiffany set the withered potato on one of the plates and took my arm. "Shall we go?" she offered brightly. Her mouth was spread wide, and her teeth were clenched together in a forced, artificial smile. "And if you say another word about this dinner, I will never speak to you again."

I laughed. "You are very convincing. I've already forgotten about it."

I helped her into the car, and we started down the mountain, neither of us talking much at first. "You're quiet tonight," she commented after a long silence.

"You threatened me back there," I responded. "I wasn't sure if I dared say anything."

She laughed softly. "I am sorry about dinner. Did I ever tell you that I'm not the world's greatest cook?"

"No," I answered slowly, "that hasn't come up in any of our conversations. But you sure gave me irrefutable proof tonight." Tiffany backhanded my arm, and I couldn't contain my laughter. She stared straight ahead, fighting to keep a straight face, but soon she cracked up too.

When we both finally settled down, Tiffany asked, "Is my disastrous dinner the only reason for you being so quiet?"

I grinned and shook my head. "No. Actually, you took my breath away."

"I took your breath away?" She sounded a little incredulous. "With dinner?"

I quickly shook my head. "No. It was you. I mean, this isn't exactly like most of the service projects that I've been on." She smiled coyly and bit down on her lower lip—a habit I suddenly realized I adored. "I mean, shoot, I've never seen you like this." My playfulness suddenly gave way to nerves and I gulped, rapidly adding, "I mean, I've seen you when you've looked nice. I mean, you know, you looked all right the night of homecoming and everything." I was practically stuttering, but I rushed on. "I'm not saying that, but tonight you . . ." I inhaled deeply. "Well, tonight you took my breath away."

Tiffany laughed, reached over, and slipped her hand through my arm as I drove. "I was hoping that you'd notice that I looked different than I do when I'm playing volleyball or helping you muck out your barn. I guess I should have paid more attention to dinner than how I looked."

"No, I'd rather skip the dinner and have you look the way you do." I shrugged. "I definitely noticed you were different tonight. I think it's that you don't have mud on your hands and dirt smudges on your cheeks and sweat dripping off your chin." I laughed.

We stopped at a little hamburger place just down the canyon and got something to eat. We ate in the car, doing our best not to get mustard and catsup all over ourselves. Then we went to the dance where we danced and talked, and I found myself quickly falling under Tiffany's intriguing charm. I forgot everything else, cognizant only of her and the fact that she was with me. When she had first asked me to the dance, I had assumed we would leave early, but we ended up staying until the end.

After leaving the dance, we drove around for a while; I suppose I wanted to prolong the night indefinitely. When we finally decided to head home, I drove down Washington Boulevard. Since it was late, there was very little traffic and the sidewalks were empty.

"Do you ever get an urge to window-shop?" Tiffany mused, glancing out the car window.

"It hasn't ever been on my list of ten exciting things to do before I die."

"Look at those sidewalks. Completely empty! Usually everything is so crowded. But you could go out there now and have the whole place to yourself. No one bumping or shoving you." She took a deep breath. "I've just got this pestering urge to window-shop."

On a sudden, wild impulse, I whipped over to the curb, parked the car, and turned off the engine. "Let's go shopping," I announced casually, opening my door.

Tiffany grinned. "I hope you're not bluffing. I really am in the mood. It will probably be a little chilly out there, and I didn't bring a coat."

"Good," I retorted. "The cold will drive us back to the car before the boredom does."

She laughed. "I'll endure the cold fine."

"We'll see how long you last," I challenged, stepping from the car and opening her door.

We must have been an odd sight in our dance finery, strolling along Ogden's downtown sidewalks well past midnight. Tiffany hugged my arm and pushed up against me to stay warm as we walked casually, admiring the clothes, the crafts, the books, and the furniture displayed in the various windows. The lights twinkled and blinked around us.

"What are we looking for?" Tiffany questioned.

"I'm looking to get back in the car and get warm," I grumbled, trying to keep my teeth from chattering.

"Chris, get in the mood and you'll forget that you're cold. That's the magic."

"How do I get into this magic mood before hypothermia sets in? Tell me quick. I don't think I can feel my toes."

"Think up something you're shopping for—furnishing the living room, fixing the den, buying clothes for the governor's ball, preparing for a camping trip. What are we shopping for?"

"This was your bright idea. You choose."

"All right, we'll redecorate Dad's den."

"Your dad doesn't even have a den."

"We don't have any money, either. The stores are all closed. It's after midnight. This is pretend, Chris." She sounded exasperated. "Now *I'm* freezing because I'm not getting into this mood fast enough." She laughed as her teeth chattered.

I stopped and slipped out of my suit coat and threw it over her shoulders. "That feels good." She shuddered. "But what about you? You'll freeze. Then who will pack our purchases?"

I shook my head as she hugged my arm. "Don't worry, I'm into this shopping mood," I said stoically. "I can't feel a thing." I stopped and looked in a window. "That cherry-colored bookshelf would look great in the den."

"I was thinking more along the lines of a really nice oak. Oak would go perfectly with the little clock hanging in the window of the novelty shop back there."

"You're going to decorate a whole room around a clock?" I questioned dubiously. "Why not find a clock to match the cherry bookshelf?"

"Look, I'm the girl. Girls have an eye for things like this. Besides, the girl should have the last word about a room's decor."

"You mean you get to call all the shots? I'm just supposed to tag along and freeze to death?"

"No, silly, you get to pay for everything. And pack the packages to the car."

"What happened to equal rights? I'm feeling used. Besides, it's your dad's den so there needs to be a male influence on the decor."

"You get to choose which books go on the bookshelf—as long as you choose ones that I approve of. We surely can't have trashy books in Dad's den."

We played this preposterous game as we walked Ogden's deserted downtown streets, and as we did, it started to snow—at first just a few stray flakes, and then, as though someone had quietly thrown open an invisible door above us, huge heavy flakes cascaded from the sky. Even though I was freezing and getting wet, I didn't want to return to the warmth of the car, preferring instead to stay with Tiffany and continue our charade.

Finally the cold and the heavy snow conquered our adventure-some spirits, and we raced down the sidewalk for the car. At least, we ran as fast as we could with Tiffany wearing a formal and heels and trying to keep my suit coat wrapped around her shoulders.

Slipping into the car, I turned on the engine and basked in the gush of warm air from the heater. "It'll be a week before I get the feeling back in my fingers and toes," I moaned, rubbing my hands together and shivering all over. "That's assuming that I'm not frostbitten and have to have all my fingers and toes amputated."

"But we've got a good start on the den," Tiffany laughed. "Don't ruin the night by thinking of a few frosted fingers and toes. We'll have to do this again sometime."

"How about next summer? In the middle of the afternoon on a very, very hot day."

"Do you know what I feel like?" Tiffany remarked. Without waiting for me to answer, she went on. "Ice cream."

"Ice cream?" I gulped. "Why not a cup of hot chocolate?"

"There's a 7-Eleven down a few blocks that sells really good soft ice cream."

"Oh, brother," I muttered, shaking my head.

"It was just a thought. But if you really cared how I felt . . ." she teased.

"Hey, the last thing I want you to do is go home and complain to your mom that I didn't get you everything you wanted," I grumbled. "Especially after that great dinner you fixed me. You know, the one I can't talk about. But if we get home late and your mom gets on my case, you tell her that this whole thing was your fault."

We found the 7-Eleven, but the ice-cream machine had been dismantled and cleaned for the night. We ended up buying ice-cream sandwiches and one steaming cup of hot chocolate. The clerk, a big man with a barrel chest, a bald head, and a tattoo that covered his entire forearm, studied our formal attire, the ice-cream sandwiches, and the hot chocolate. "Big night on the town?" he questioned with raised eyebrows. His nose twitched and he added, "I usually took my date to a nice restaurant after a big dance."

I looked at the clerk, somewhat taken aback. Tiffany burst out laughing. She whispered loudly to him, "I had to twist his arm to buy the ice-cream sandwiches. And we've got to share the cup of hot chocolate. McDonald's is the fanciest place he's ever taken me."

"Hey, buddy," the clerk grumbled, folding his arms across his chest, "we're running a sale on hot dogs, two for a buck and a quarter." He nodded once and then dug into his own pocket, pulled out a quarter, two dimes, and a few pennies, and slapped them on the counter. "I'll even help you pay. It's not McDonald's, but what the heck, it's a meal. Don't take her home hungry."

We bought the two hot dogs. The clerk gave us—on the house— another cup of hot chocolate. Then we sat in the car and ate our late-night snack while the snow continued to fall all around us.

When we finally did start up the mountain to Eden, the roads were covered with snow and we could see only a few feet ahead of us. I was relieved when we finally pulled into Tiffany's driveway. Using my suit coat as an umbrella for both of us, I escorted Tiffany through the snow to her front porch. She clung to my arm and shivered against the cold, pressing against me while her hair tickled my face and neck. At the door she pulled away and faced me. We stood for a moment under the porch light, both of us shaking, our teeth chattering.

"Thanks," she beamed. "I hope you're glad you went."

"Shoot," I said, shrugging as I shook the snow from my coat and slipped it on. "I got a whole plate of brownies out of the deal." I grinned, trembling from the cold. "It was worth it."

Tiffany laughed, her eyes catching the golden glint from the porch light. "I've had a crazy, wonderful time, Chris." She reached out, snatched my hand, and shook it in a clownish kind of way. "Thanks again and good night," she added stiffly, formally.

"A handshake?" I protested. "I thought I'd get a hug," I chided her playfully. "Or at least another plate of brownies." My teeth chattered slightly as I spoke.

Suddenly Tiffany dropped my hand, threw her arms around me, and pulled me close in a tight embrace. Her unexpected move shocked me, but before I could recover, she stepped back, put both her hands on my chest, and shoved me away. "Now go home before you freeze to death, you silly boy. There's a blizzard out here. And I think I hear my dad coming." She laughed. "I don't want him to catch you here this late. He'll break your legs and twist your head off. Then how will we finish furnishing the den?" In one quick movement, she turned and slipped inside the house, leaving me standing under the porch light.

"She would have kissed Brad," I said out loud, kidding with myself. I stepped off the porch and started back to the car. Halfway there I stopped and stared at the Bronco we had just driven up in. *Tiffany's car!* Obviously she had forgotten that we had driven in her car. I glanced back toward the house. There were no lights on and there was no way that I was going to knock or ring the bell and ask Tiffany to drive me home. So, shrugging and shaking my head, I started home through the heavily falling snow.

CHAPTER SEVEN

Saturday morning I slept in. At least, I slept in until Lisa barged into my room and shoved the cordless phone in my face as I lay on my pillow. "It's for you," she announced.

I stared blearily at the clock on the dresser. "It's barely seven o'clock," I muttered, rubbing my eyes and pushing up on an elbow. I glared at the phone on my pillow. "Who the heck . . ." I took the phone and put it to my ear without saying anything, just moaning slightly.

"Have you seen it?" Tiffany's voice crackled with enthusiasm. "You're going, aren't you? There's no way we can miss this."

"I think you've got the wrong number," I muttered, closing my eyes and flopping back on my pillow. "Besides, I think it's a felony to call someone on a Saturday morning before noon. I hope you've got a really good lawyer."

"You big, dumb lump of laziness. Get out of bed and look outside."

"Oh, Tiffany," I said, trying to sound surprised. "I didn't know this was you. Hey, thanks for making me walk home in a blizzard last night. That was way too cool. Did you plan that or did it just work out that way? After you burned my dinner, I didn't think things could get any worse. You proved me wrong."

There was a brief silence on the other end of the line. I heard her clear her throat. "You walked home in the snow?" she asked slowly.

"Well, I considered waiting on your porch for a while, thinking that you'd probably remember that you were the one who had asked me to the dance and that it was your car we went in and that you'd come down and give me a ride home. But I finally gave up on that idea. It's probably good I did because I'd still be there waiting for you, wouldn't I? Of course, I'd be a little blue and really stiff, but . . ."

"Oh, Chris, I'm so sorry," she soothed, and then she burst out laughing. "Chris, I'm sorry. I really am."

"Yeah, your remorse is overpowering."

"But we can't do anything about that now, Chris. Don't be a big baby. Get over it, because we've got other things to think about now. Have you looked outside?"

"Tiffany, I haven't even gotten out of bed. In fact, I wouldn't even be awake right now except that you called me. You'd be tired too if you spent a night trudging through a blizzard because you were stranded."

"Stop complaining and go to the window and look outside."

Kicking my covers off, I stumbled from the bed and staggered to the window. I pulled back the curtains and gazed out. The whole world was white, dotted by a few dark fence posts and barren bushes and trees. There must have been at least ten inches of new snow on the ground. The skies were overcast, and thick flakes continued to fall steadily and noiselessly to the ground.

"Are you looking?"

"It snowed. A whole bunch."

"So you're going, right?"

"Going where?" I asked, walking unsteadily back to my bed where I crashed tiredly.

"Didn't you see? Nobody has even stepped in it."

"Let's see how long we can leave it that way."

"Chris!"

"Tiffany, it's Saturday morning. Everybody's in bed. And now that it's snowed, everybody's got a perfect excuse to stay in bed for the rest of the day. Including me!"

"Nobody's played in the snow. I don't even see anybody shoveling their driveways."

I laughed. "That's what I've been trying to tell you—everybody's asleep."

"You're hopeless," she muttered. "I'm going for a walk. Alone, if I have to."

I laughed again. "Where are you going?" There was a pause. "I'm just curious," I quickly added.

"I'll be making footsteps in the snow." She stopped. "Put on your boots, you lazy bum. And dress warm, because we'll probably be gone for a long time."

"I'm still in bed, Tiffany."

"If you're still in bed when I get there, I'll tromp all over you with my boots." She abruptly hung up without even asking if I was really going with her. Most likely she knew I would be unable to resist her wild invitation.

Complaining to myself the whole while, I dug out my boots and bundled up in a pair of pants, two sweatshirts, a coat, a woolen cap, and gloves. Just as I was pulling on my gloves, Tiffany hammered on the front door. "I guess there's no sense in pointing out to you that this is insane," I stated dryly, stepping out to join her, flapping my arms a couple of times before actually venturing into the deep sea of white that had engulfed our world overnight.

"You're such a baby, Chris," she chided, puffs of steam coming from her nose and mouth. She was bundled in layers of sweaters, pants, a puffy red parka, boots, thick gloves, and a bright orange scarf that was wrapped about her neck and tied under her chin. Only her eyes, nose, and mouth were unexposed. Her blue eyes watered and sparkled in the cold. Her nose was red. "Think of this as an adventure, an adventure that's only going to be available for a few more minutes. If we don't make tracks right now," she said with a sweep of her arm, "somebody will beat us to it." She threw her head back and laughed. Grabbing my arm, she charged off the porch. I stumbled and tipped off balance. Before I could recover and steady myself, Tiffany charged into me with her shoulder, knocking me into the snow. She laughed raucously.

The two of us raced recklessly into the white, virgin wilderness. We headed down the road, but it had already been spoiled by several tire tracks, so Tiffany insisted we cut into the fields where the blanket of white was unmarred.

Tiffany's playful exuberance was contagious. Before long I was tromping, running, kicking, rolling, and stumbling in the white, crunchy, icy fluffiness. We threw it, ate it, and fell in it. Soon we were both snow-covered, looking like two walking snowmen. We wandered aimlessly, and that's how we finally ended up at the garden; this particular morning we were consciously searching for isolated spots, untouched by any living thing, and the garden was off by itself—a natural destination, however unplanned it might have been.

"This is the garden?" Tiffany muttered in surprise, squinting against the glare of the brilliant white snow.

The garden was an isolated two-acre patch of rich, black ground, cloistered at the bottom of the western mountains and surrounded by brush-covered ridges. According to Grandpa Huish, it was great farmland, some of the best in the valley. He had developed it years earlier, clearing off the brush, digging out the rocks, and carving a ditch between two adjoining ridges to give the ground a drink from the irrigation canal. The garden was too small and inaccessible for a crop like hay or barley, so it had become his garden, pampered and preened in his spare time, but also eventually abandoned because it was too far from the rest of the fields.

Years later, while repairing a fence line, Brad and I had discovered the garden, overgrown with brush, grass, and weeds. We didn't even know that it was part of the farm until Dad told us. It piqued our youthful imaginations, and we decided to become rich by raising watermelons. Dad didn't exactly encourage us, but he did say that it might work; Grandpa had always claimed that since the garden was low and protected on all sides by those ridges, it would escape the late spring freezes so common in the valley.

Brad and I spent a whole spring preparing the garden spot— digging weeds, hauling rocks away, cleaning out the ditch down the hill from the irrigation canal, tilling the ground, and hauling in manure. All the while we dreamed of how fantastic it would be to have tons of watermelons to eat and sell. On occasion, Tiffany even gave us a hand. We never actually planted anything. By the time we were finished preparing the ground, it was too late to plant. We told ourselves that we'd start earlier the next year, but by the next year, we had become disillusioned and had abandoned the dream.

Now as Tiffany stood in this small, bowl-shaped valley surrounded on all sides by low, round, marshmallow-like hills, I answered her inquiry, "Yeah, this is the garden."

"I was thinking it was farther that way." She pointed to the northwest and rubbed her nose with the back of an icy glove. "It looks different than I remember it," she said seriously.

I tossed my head back and laughed. "There wasn't ten feet of snow here when we were working on it." I gave her a hard shove, and she tumbled into the snow.

She sat up and looked around. I held a hand out to help her up, but she ignored it, seemingly intrigued by this isolated spot. Although Tiffany had worked in the garden some, she had been the pragmatic one, telling us that watermelons probably weren't the ideal crop for the Huntsville Valley. She suggested something dull and lame like wheat, corn, or barley.

"It'll be a while before we start planting watermelons, won't it?" she teased, picking up a handful of snow, pressing it into a ball, and tossing it at my head. I ducked it easily. "Now if you could grow a really good crop of watermelons here, that might impress Professor Hill." Lawrence Hill was our Advanced Botany teacher, a pedantic man referred to by most students at Weber High as "Professor." "The illustrious Professor would give you an A for sure."

I chuckled in amusement. "Imagine growing watermelons on this very spot. Now that would be a stroke of scientific genius. Wouldn't that freak the Professor out?" I shook my head. "Shoot! That'd freak everybody out, including me."

Tiffany began methodically digging with her gloved hands, making small, bowl-shaped holes in the snow in a straight line. "What are you doing?" I asked skeptically.

She gave me a look of pure innocence. "Planting watermelons, of course. I hope you didn't forget the seeds."

I patted my pocket. "Right here. I knew you'd want to plant just before the spring thaw."

"Are you going to stand around and let me do all the work?" She paused for a moment and gazed around her. "You know," she mused slowly, "crisp, cold watermelon will have a whole new meaning when these melons come up. I wonder if they'll be red or white." She fought off the temptation to laugh. "Aren't you going to help me?" she asked again.

"Yeah, I'm going to help you," I burst out. "I'm going to help push your head into that hole you're digging. Then I'm going to cover you with about a ton of snow."

Soon we were throwing and kicking snow at each other. And before long we were panting, gasping, and laughing. Finally we dropped into the snow and stared up at the gray sky. We lay there without speaking.

"What *do* you think about growing watermelons here?" Tiffany asked. This time she was genuinely serious. "Would it have worked?"

I smiled wanly, pondering a moment. "I think you might be able to pull it off." I looked over at her. "I mean, we'd have to let the snow melt and all." I grinned. "But I don't think Brad and I were too far off the mark."

"Would this qualify for the 'super project' in Professor Hill's class?" She stood up, brushed at her pants and coat, and then held out a hand.

I let her pull me up. "Maybe." I brushed at my own pants and coat. "If we wrote up the proposal just right. Of course, we wouldn't see the end product until well into summer, a long time after the class was over, but we could do all the preliminary work and write up the plans and make predictions and stuff like that."

"We could do it together," Tiffany volunteered.

I smiled. "You're half serious, aren't you?"

She shook her head. "No, I'm all the way serious. We've got to turn our proposals in Friday, and I don't have a clue what I'm going to do. This is as good as anything."

I looked around. "We'd have to take a picture of the place today so the professor would know what we were dealing with." I grinned and nudged Tiffany.

"I'm serious, Chris. We ought to do it." A smile tugged at her lips. "Of course, I'd get half the profit. I certainly wouldn't do this solely for academic reasons."

"So it's the money that's motivating you?" I joked, surveying the white field in front of us. Although a few flakes continued to fall, the snow had almost stopped. "Do you think we ought to plant a few pineapples?" I mused thoughtfully. "Just for variety," I quickly added, pressing my lips together to bite off the threatening smile. "And as long as we're planting pineapples, what about a few mango and coconut trees? We could change this into a regular tropical paradise."

Tiffany lowered her shoulder and drove into my side, knocking me off balance. Before I could recover, she slammed into me again and sent me sprawling in the snow. "That will teach you to make fun of my botany project." She turned and started running. "I'm heading home. I'm frozen," she flung over her shoulder. "If you can beat me, I'll fix you a cup of hot cocoa."

It took us thirty minutes to reach Tiffany's place because we kept tripping and knocking each other down in the snow. We were soaked, shivering, and a bit numb by the time we took off our coats and sweaters and walked in stocking feet into the Gibson kitchen. Tiffany started heating water for the hot cocoa while I got two cups from the cupboard, a couple of spoons from the utensil drawer, and a bag of miniature marshmallows from the pantry.

"After last night's dinner," I questioned, "don't you think I ought to heat that water? I don't know if you can scorch water, but you might manage without even trying."

Using a spoon, she flicked hot water at me. "You were supposed to forget about last night's dinner, Chris. Give it a rest."

A few minutes later we held our cups of hot cocoa, blowing gently across the brown liquid where white marshmallow dots bobbed. After a few gingerly sips, Tiffany set her cup on the table, stood, and left the room. She returned with a yellow notepad and a black felt-tip pen. "All right," she said, sitting down. "What's the first thing we've got to do?"

With my cup still in front of my face, the faint traces of steam curling up before my nose and eyes, I squinted at her and inquired, "What are you talking about?"

She set her pen down and stared across the table at me. "The watermelon patch." She picked up the pen again. "You're the farmer. What do we need to do first?"

I set my cup down and tried not to break into a laugh. "Probably the first thing we should do is . . ." I fought back the impulse to smile. "The first thing we should do," I started again, "is to take a quick reality check. What planet did you say you're from?"

"Very funny."

I shook my head. "Well, then, maybe the first thing we should do is order the pineapples. They're harder to come by. It might take a few months for them to arrive. Then we could—"

"I'm waiting," she cut in, tapping her pen on the notepad. She cupped her chin in her hand and put her elbow on the table. "And if you get smart with me, I'm going to dump that hot chocolate down your back."

"You can't be serious."

"About the watermelons, or pouring the cocoa down your back?"

"Both."

"Dead serious. That watermelon patch is my botany project. What do we have to do?"

"The smartest thing to do is not to plant watermelons," I stated simply.

"Chris, this cocoa is really hot!" she threatened.

I heaved an exasperated sigh. "The one thing Brad and I did right when we came up with this brainchild was never plant the watermelons. Now drink your cocoa."

Undaunted, Tiffany continued to badger me until I started to plan haphazardly. At first I just said stuff, brainstorming without really being serious. "If we grow melons up here, we have to have a hotbed so that by the time we actually plant them in the garden they've been growing for a month or so."

"How many plants?"

"To make it profitable, we'd have to have three or four hundred."

"Four hundred." She was writing. "What kind of a hotbed will handle four hundred plants?"

It was crazy—a bit reminiscent of our window-shopping caper the night before—but we worked into the afternoon at Tiffany's kitchen table, planning, writing, organizing, speculating, and fantasizing until I began to believe that we might even be able to pull this project off. Tiffany's crazy, ridiculous enthusiasm had rubbed off on me.

By Friday we had put together a proposal for our botany project, complete with measurements, materials, timelines, costs, and other details. What had started out as a joke as we romped wildly in the snow became a moderately feasible botany project.

"Let's not tell Brad about this," I suggested to Tiffany one evening as we worked at her house on our botany notebook.

She looked up from her books, chewing pensively on the end of a pencil. "Why's that?"

I shrugged, considering for a moment. "When Brad and I planned this a few years back, we both finally decided it wouldn't work." I smiled faintly. I pulled on my earlobe and shrugged. "I'd just like to surprise him."

I started considering ideas again, and my eyes narrowed as I stared absentmindedly at a spot on the wall just above Tiffany's head. "If we have the hotbeds ready by the end of March and get everything planted the first part of April, it might work. We'll have to have heaters and blowers going in those hotbeds at night because it can freeze up here clear into May. But if we can get the melon plants out of the hotbeds and into the garden by the middle of May, and if the weather cooperates a little, we're going to have local watermelons up here the first part of August."

"How do you keep all of this a secret from Brad?"

"He's not home much, and we'll put the hotbeds on the west side of the barn. He won't even be able to see them from the house." I grinned. "We'll keep him from wandering around if he comes home on the weekend." I laughed. "It'll blow him away to know that we actually did it."

* * *

Most Saturdays and many evenings over the next several weeks, we worked in the barn, building the frames for the hotbeds. We laid the beds out, and stretched heavy, clear plastic over them. We experimented with heaters and blowers to regulate the temperature once the hotbeds were built and in place.

One evening as I was going out the door to drive to Ogden with Tiffany—to pick up the watermelon seeds—my younger brother Randy asked innocently, "You kinda like Tiffany, don't you?" He said it like it was a new discovery for him. I stopped at the open door and faced him. He lay on the living room sofa, a cushion propped under his head while he hugged a second one in his arms. "She's like your girlfriend."

I laughed. "Tiffany, Brad, and I have been friends forever."

He punched the cushion on his chest. "I'm just saying that it's different now."

I smiled patiently. "And what makes it so different now?"

"How should I know? You should tell *me* what makes it different."

"You're letting your imagination run away with you."

"So you don't like her—like a girlfriend, I mean?"

"What are you, the neighborhood attorney cross-examining everybody that passes through here?" I shook my head. "Don't think too deeply, big guy. You're liable to blow a brain fuse." Laughing, I slipped out the door, but I didn't completely forget what Randy had pointed out to me.

CHAPTER EIGHT

Tiffany and I seeded the watermelon pots in the hotbeds the first Saturday in April. Previously we had spent hours in the barn mixing common dirt, sand, potting soil, manure, and mulch so that we could fill the four hundred pots. We had also ordered and received hybrid watermelon seeds.

"Will it work?" Tiffany asked, surveying our dirt before seeding the pots.

"It works on paper," I answered, grinning and rubbing the back of my neck as we worked in the barn. "At least it should pull us an A in botany. The Professor was definitely impressed with our notebook."

It was dark before we finally had all the pots planted, watered, and placed inside the hotbeds, and everything tied down securely as the heaters and fans circulated the warm air. When we were convinced that things were as stable as we could get them, we went inside. Our fantastic watermelon project was clearly past the paper-and-pencil stage.

Once the watermelons were planted, we didn't do much except maintain the temperature and make sure the plants were watered regularly. I did most of that because Tiffany was involved in track, competing in the 100- and 200-meters and anchoring the 400-meter relay team. I saw her at school from time to time, but other than that we didn't have much time for each other.

A week after we planted, Brad called to give the family a report on spring drills and practice. "The first week is always rough because you're rusty and trying to get your rhythm back—but," he announced enthusiastically, "but it was weird, like everything I did was oiled and smooth. I could just feel something different. Everything I did worked like a charm."

"Did the coach have the same impressions?" I kidded him.

Brad laughed. "You're a real cynic, Chris. Have a little faith in me. If you want to know the truth, everybody was struggling. I have worked out a lot, but still I should have been the rusty one—I mean, shoot, I missed most of last season. Instead, it was like somebody was helping me, making sure that every pass, every move, was right on the money. I could have beat anybody this week. Man, I could have played for the pros," he hooted excitedly.

"Don't book a ticket for San Francisco just yet," I razzed him. "Wait for the 49ers to call you. Besides, you really ought to play one season at Snow before you bust into the pro ranks. I guess this means you'd better tell the bishop to put your missionary papers in a drawer."

There was a brief pause. "Yeah. I guess so." He cleared his throat. "They're all ready to go, too. All the bishop has to do is send them to the stake president."

We finished our conversation on that uncertain note, and a week later Brad called again. We joked for a few minutes, and he asked how my training for the marathon was progressing.

"About the same as before."

"So you're jogging four or five miles every morning?"

I chuckled. "Three or four times a week I'll go out for a jog. Not in the mornings, though. It's still too cold up here for that. But day before yesterday I ran four miles. I wasn't sucking air too bad when I got back."

"You'll have to build up to more than four miles, kid," he told me. "And you'll need to run every single day. You can take Sundays off. Remember, that marathon's coming up fast."

"I'll keep that in mind," I said lightly. "I'll make sure I get that marathon date on my calendar. I sure as heck don't want to miss that."

There was a long pause. I was expecting Brad to continue to harass me, but he surprised me. "The bishop sent my papers to the stake president."

His comment didn't register for a moment. "He did what?" I stammered, clutching the phone. "Why did he do that? He can't just send them off like that without your permission."

"He got my permission."

For a long moment neither one of us said anything. "What about football?" I finally managed to ask. "Did everything just go belly-up out there on the field?"

"I quit the team," he said quietly. "I have a part-time job starting Monday. It'll change to full-time at the end of the semester. I could have my call in a few weeks." He coughed. "I figured you should be the first to know."

"I don't get it," I mumbled, clearly confused. "I mean, you were so sure about football." I shook my head, wondering momentarily if he was messing with my mind. "You're not just giving me a bunch of Bradley bull, are you?"

"I'm going on a mission," he returned softly. "That's what I want to do. *You* changed my mind."

"Me? What did I do?"

"You were always sure about your mission. I wanted to be that sure too."

* * *

The next day Tiffany stopped by after track to check on our watermelon project. After showing her how things were going, I remarked, "Brad quit football." She looked over at me, obviously shocked. "He's going on a mission," I explained.

Suddenly she clenched both her fists, held them up, and burst out, "Way to go, Brad!" She squealed enthusiastically and backhanded me on the shoulder, then pressed her lips together, deep in thought. "I know we were going to split the watermelon profits between the two of us, but what do you say we split it three ways?"

I smiled faintly. "And cut Brad in?" I asked knowingly.

"He could use the money for his mission." She grinned broadly and shook her head. "No, I'll do even better than that. Fifty percent for your mission, fifty percent for Brad's."

I laughed and decided to tease her. "Or he could use his fifty percent to get you a ring."

Tiffany's cheeks turned a bright, embarrassed pink. "While Brad's on his mission," I added, "I'll plant another patch of watermelons for the ring." I laughed and turned away, and as I did, she gave me a hard kick in the seat of my pants. As I whipped around to face her, still holding my behind, she wagged her finger in my face and scolded lightheartedly, "I don't know how many times I have told you this, but I'm going to tell you again—I should have never, ever told you any of that about Brad. You just like to torment me." She stuffed her hands into her back pockets. "But you can forget it. I've decided not to marry Brad. I've realized that I'm probably just infatuated with him. I'm going to marry someone else."

"Without even consulting Brad? Brad might be counting on you to hang around for him," I taunted her. "After all, he's put up with you all these years. He probably feels that he's got to marry you."

"Well," she sighed, "I guess he'll just have to get over those notions, won't he?"

"So who's the other lucky guy? I mean, this new one that you're going to marry?"

She gave me a narrow-eyed, withering glare. "You, Mr. Christopher Can't-Keep-His-Big-Mouth-Shut Huish, are the very *last* person in the whole wide world that I would ever share that information with. I will never tell you another secret as long as I live. Probably even longer than that."

"Does that mean I'm not getting an invitation to your wedding?" I asked, trying to appear hurt.

"Exactly."

"So even though you're not going to marry Brad, you still want to give him your portion of the melon patch for his mission?"

"Yes. This project is not just a botany project—it's a missionary project, too."

I jabbed a finger in her direction. "We still don't tell Brad anything, not until those plants are growing in the garden. The last thing we need is to tell him that we've dedicated this whole watermelon patch to his mission and then have a frost come along and wipe everything out. It would be like him dedicating one of his football games to us and then losing it big time!"

One Saturday morning near the end of April, I was sleeping in when Mom knocked on my door, pushed it open a crack, and called to me, "Brad's going to Culiacán, Mexico. He enters the MTC the first part of July."

My eyes flashed wide and my mouth dropped open. "He's got his call already? I wasn't expecting it for another week or two."

She laughed excitedly and stepped into the bedroom as I sat up in bed. She smiled. "He had planned to open it here with us, but when I called him and told him that it was here, he was so excited he couldn't wait. He insisted that I open the envelope right then."

After that news, I couldn't sleep any longer. I got out of bed, showered, ate some toast, and headed to the hotbeds. As I came around the corner of the barn, I collided with Tiffany.

"Why are you sleeping away your whole day?" she accused, nodding in the direction of the hotbeds. She grinned and burst into a laugh. "What do you think about Brad's call? Mexico!"

"Mom told you?" I asked, feeling a tinge of disappointment in not being the one to break the news to her.

"Brad called me. I almost told him our secret," she added, shaking her head and blushing. "But I bit my tongue. As soon as I hung up the phone, I charged over here to work on the mission melons." She sighed happily. "Nothing's going to go wrong with this melon project now."

After Brad's announcement, the days rushed by. There were papers to write, tests to study for, and projects to finish. Tiffany did well in track. At regionals, she ended up taking first in the 200-meter and second in the 100-meter, which qualified her for state. She was also on the relay team that took first in the region meet. I continued to run almost every day but still had no desire to run a marathon.

The watermelon project consumed our spare moments. The conditions in the hotbeds were ideal, and the tiny plants thrived. By the first of May we were beginning to worry that they would mature before we could get them transplanted into the garden.

We knew we had to get the ground ready, so Dad helped us get the old tractor running and we hitched up the plow. We found it tricky maneuvering the big, bulky tractor down the narrow lane leading to the garden, but we managed.

It had been more than three years since Brad and I first cleared the garden spot so there was still a considerable amount of work to do to get the ground ready. The plot was grown over. Tiffany and I spent two Saturdays and several evenings burning off the weeds and dry grass and hauling away the rocks that the plow dug up. We disked and harrowed the ground until the rich, black soil begged to be planted.

"You've got to make a decision, Chris," Dad counseled me. "If you leave the plants in the hotbeds much longer, they'll start to die. They need to be in the ground."

"It's too early to put them in the garden though," I said, wincing. "We could still get early morning frosts."

Dad pondered. "It's been a mild spring. I suggest you take a gamble." He scratched his head. "Besides, the garden is pretty well protected down among those hills. Grandpa always said that it was the last place in the whole valley to freeze. I say plant now and hope he was right."

Following Dad's advice, we transplanted on the second Saturday in May. We were up at five o'clock in the morning, and Dad and Randy helped us. We didn't have access to irrigation that early in the year, so we had to haul water down in barrels to do the transplanting.

It was growing dark when we finally put the last tender plant in the ground. Dad and Randy had left earlier to finish chores at the house, so Tiffany and I were left to finish the garden alone. I sucked in a long breath and exhaled slowly as I surveyed the melon patch in the diminishing light. "They look pretty fragile out there," I muttered.

Tiffany nudged my arm with her elbow. "They'll make it. They're mission melons."

"I just hope mission melons can withstand a good, hard frost if one comes." I turned and glanced at her as she stared dreamily out across the garden. Her face was streaked and smudged with dirt and sweat. Her reddish-blond hair drooped down over her eyes and tumbled out from under her black Raiders cap. Her hands were dirty and her knees caked with dried mud from kneeling and crawling on the ground. She looked wilted and exhausted, but her eyes were still bright and happy. And she was beautiful. That surprised me. It was strange, but as she stood there in her dirty bib overalls and ragged flannel shirt, she reminded me of how she looked the night of the Sweetheart Dance. Although her appearance now was radically different from that night, she was still beautiful. I recalled Randy's simple observation several weeks ago about Tiffany being my girlfriend. As I looked at her now, I began to wonder if I hoped he was right.

"Where's your faith?" Tiffany chided me. She bumped me with her hip and jabbed her elbow into my side. "It's been warm today, and it's not supposed to get cold tonight."

"As long as they were in the hotbeds, we could watch them, adjust the temperature, water them, take care of them." I shook my head. "They're on their own now, and I want something to show Brad when he returns home."

"By the time he comes home, we'll have watermelons."

"Maybe I ought to camp out here tonight," I suggested, turning back to the melon patch.

Tiffany laughed. "Chris, if it's going to freeze, it'll freeze whether you're here or not." She sighed pensively. "But camping out might be fun." She looked at me out of the corners of her eyes. "Shall we camp out? Like old times?" She burst out laughing. "We're probably past that stage, aren't we?" She took my hand and tugged on it. "Let's head home. I want a long, hot bath—then I want to crawl into bed and not wake up for about two weeks."

Even though both our hands were dirty, I let her lead me by the hand out of the garden. We walked most of the way up the dirt trail before Tiffany finally let my hand go, returning to her house.

I usually slept in Sunday morning until just before church, but I got up early the next day, climbed into the Chevy, and headed out to the garden. I left the window down just to see how cold it was outside. There was a definite chill in the air. I parked the truck at the top of the lane by the dry irrigation canal and jogged down to the garden, afraid to look until I was right there.

As I rounded the last turn in the lane, the garden stretched in front of me, the sun shining brightly on the long, straight rows of small watermelon plants. They were green and beautiful and even more perky than they had appeared the day before. "Thanks," I voiced in a quiet prayer, gazing up momentarily at the blue sky. "We made it through the first night."

I wandered up and down the rows, feeling a keen sense of satisfaction, knowing that there wasn't another watermelon plant in the whole valley as far along as these. In fact, there wouldn't be watermelon plants this far along until the middle of June or later, and since early fall frosts were common in the valley, the chances of anyone else up here producing ripe watermelons before the first frost were slim.

"Who said we can't grow watermelons in the valley?" I said softly. "I might try pineapple next year."

As I walked to the top of the patch, I kept my head down, examining the plants as I went. "They survived," a voice called to me.

I looked up. Tiffany stood at the top of the rows in a denim jumper with her hands on her hips and a huge grin on her face. Her hair was wet and she didn't have any makeup on. The sun was to her back, giving her head and shoulders a glowing red halo. "You got nervous too?" I questioned, grinning sheepishly.

"I got out of the shower and saw the Chevy go around the corner. I knew it had to be you headed this way. So I hopped on my bike to join you. You can't have all the fun to yourself."

"What happened to the two-week sleep you were craving last night?"

She shrugged. "I guess it's the farmer in me." She giggled. "Are you staying here all day, or do you think you'll tear yourself away and go to church?"

I looked back at the patch and then glanced at the blue sky, letting the sun's growing warmth soak through my shirt. "They'll be all right today." I smiled. "I guess I'll go to church."

When we returned to the Chevy, I tossed Tiffany's bike into the back. "We won't get our first irrigation turn for another two weeks," I pointed out. "Do you know what that means?"

She reached over and playfully checked my left biceps. "I hope your momma is feeding you really good, because you're going to have to pack a whole lot of water in the next two weeks." Squeezing my biceps again, she joked, "You seem pretty stout though. And I'll check on you every now and then to give you some words of encouragement. You'll make it."

I shook her hand off my arm. "Hey, this is *our* project."

"You don't expect me to haul all that water."

"Only half of it."

"What kind of a gentleman are you?" she teased, raising her eyebrows and cocking her head to one side.

"Do you remember that day back in February?" I jabbed a forefinger in her direction. "You were the one hounding me about planting watermelons. Well, they're planted. There's still work to do."

"I think I liked it better when the garden was covered with about a foot of snow."

Most afternoons after school, Tiffany and I drove the old Chevy to the garden with three 50-gallon drums of water loaded in the back, sloshing liquid every which way. It took us three afternoons to water the entire patch. Then it seemed as though we had to turn right around and start over again the next day. After watering each evening, we hit our books to study. It was a horrible work schedule, and we didn't have a choice. But it ended up being rather fun, even if it was backbreaking at times.

Twice during the two weeks after transplanting, temperatures in the valley dipped low. Both nights there were several reports of freezing throughout the valley. Each morning after those cold nights, Tiffany and I drove to the garden to assess the damage. Oddly, each time, we found the watermelon plants thriving in spite of the cold in other places.

Once, after returning from an early morning inspection of the garden, I found Dad at the breakfast table finishing a bowl of cold cereal. "How do your watermelons look?" he asked, looking up. "Did the frost hit them?"

"Well," I answered, sitting across the table from him, "apparently the watermelon plants looked fine. Before going out there this morning, Tiffany talked to her neighbors—Mrs. Harvey and Mrs. Reynolds—and both of them said their tomato plants were hit last night, so I know it was cold, but none of the watermelons in the garden were touched."

Dad shook his head and smiled. "I don't know what it is, but there's something about the garden's location that protects that little piece of ground. Your grandpa claimed that it took a hard freeze in the valley before the frost hit the garden. I always figured it was his imagination, but maybe he was right."

"Well," I remarked, nodding, "there must be something, because this is the second freeze since we transplanted, and those melon plants haven't been touched yet. Of course, we haven't had any hard frosts, but there's still been some freezing in the valley. We're keeping our fingers crossed, but we're also banking on what Grandpa claimed."

One evening Tiffany and I trudged from the garden after spending two hours carrying water to the small plants. Our hands were muddy, our backs aching. "I was just thinking," Tiffany said tiredly, "you could send your missionary papers in anytime now."

I smiled, a little surprised. "You know, I hadn't thought about that. I guess I've been worrying about everything else. Like not flunking Government and English, graduating with the rest of the class, planting watermelons, and a few other minor details." I chuckled, slapping at the dirt on my pants. "I just haven't felt old enough to be sending my missionary papers off."

"You're going to send them off soon, aren't you?"

I glanced at my watch. "Probably not tonight. I think I can wait at least one more day."

"But you will, won't you?" she persisted.

I breathed deeply. "It depends," I responded with overt casualness. "I'll have to see how the watermelons turn out. If we have a good crop and make lots of money, then maybe I'll talk to the bishop. Unless, of course, I decide to use the money on a new car. I saw one when I—"

Tiffany cut me off with a stern look. "Look, for your information," she answered quietly, suddenly serious, "I can't take any of that back-and-forth thing Brad went through. So stop whining and turn them in. I want to stop worrying about them."

"Worrying?" I remarked flippantly. "Tiffany, I didn't know you *cared*. Why didn't you tell me sooner?"

She faced me. "Look, my hands are cracked and dry. I've broken three nails in the last two weeks. My back aches, and I'm getting calluses." She held up her hands. "Do you think I play farmer woman because I like this?" she asked, a wan smile on her face. "This is for your and Brad's missions. So if you're having second thoughts about a mission, you'd better tell me soon."

"Or you'll beat me up?"

She smiled deviously. "Something like that. Or worse!"

CHAPTER NINE

The last two weeks of school were a blur. I had hoped that Brad would come home at the end of his semester, but he stayed in Ephraim and worked. In fact, he planned to work there on his construction job until a week before he left for the MTC. Each time he called home, though, he exuded excitement about his mission to Mexico.

Friday afternoon, the last day of school, I drove the old Chevy pickup into the yard and spotted Brad's Civic. I parked underneath the poplar tree and stepped from the truck, feeling a surge of excitement. It had been a long time since I'd seen Brad.

"Brad's here," Randy called from the barn, where he had his bike dissected and was working on the rear wheel. "I helped him move his things into your room," he added proudly.

"Why didn't he make it last night?" I flung over my shoulder as I jogged toward the house, not really expecting an answer.

"He worked late," Randy shouted, excited to share any news about Brad. "He said I could move in with you when he leaves for the MTC. I'll take his bottom bunk."

"Don't count on it," I hollered halfway to the house. "You've got your own room."

"It's Mom's sewing room, too," he flared, shaking a wrench at me. "I'm sick of being crammed into that old sewing room."

I leaped over the four-foot-high chain-link fence surrounding our backyard, charged up the back steps, banged through the screen door into the kitchen, and almost knocked Mom over as she closed the refrigerator. "Aren't we in a hurry!" she gasped, stepping back and looking me up and down. "And I thought we had an understanding about climbing over that back fence." She wagged a spatula under my nose, but I could tell she was in a good mood.

"I didn't think you were watching. Besides, if I jump the fence, I won't wear out the gate." I grinned.

"I'm charging you every time you climb over." She rinsed her hands in the sink. "You're not excited to see anybody, are you?" She laughed and started humming softly. My eyes darted toward the stairs. "He's waiting upstairs, as crazy to see you as you are to see him," Mom said.

I took the stairs two at a time and burst in the bedroom, banging the door into the dresser. Brad lay on the bottom bunk with his head propped up by his doubled-up pillow. His hands were behind his head and his eyes were closed, but as soon as I barged into the room, they opened, and a huge grin crinkled his tan face. His dark hair was shorter than I'd seen it in a long time, trimmed missionary style. He was also darker because of the weeks he had worked construction in the sun. His blue eyes teased from under his thick brows. He hadn't shaved that morning, so he looked a bit rugged.

"Don't you ever knock?" he questioned playfully.

I kicked at his foot. "This is *my* room. And what gives you the right to tell Randy he can move in here?"

"I can promise it to whoever I want. It's still my place." He motioned about the room with a sweep of his hand. "Shoot, I plan to rent it out and make a few bucks on the side."

"For your information, you are no longer a resident in this particular room. Officially, you're now a guest. In fact, I've been meaning to box up your leftover junk and pack it out to the barn loft." I laughed and faked a punch at his chin. "After I've kept the stuff I want."

"I see you've managed to keep things clean and orderly." He looked about the room. "I did a quick inspection—no dust, things were straight even under the bed, no junk stuffed in the closet. All my excellent training over the years has finally paid off."

"*Your* training?" I snorted. "It's a cinch to keep this place clean without you here to trash it every time you walk through the door," I grumbled, pulling out the desk chair and sitting down. "You don't know how nice it is to come in here without tripping over your shoes or a pile of your sweaty, smelly shorts and socks. I hope your roommates taught you something about keeping your room clean. You sure wouldn't take any lessons from me."

Brad groaned disgustedly. "That's because you were such an obnoxious fanatic. Luckily, the guys in the dorm were all slobs, worse than I ever was. But for your information, Chris, your nagging ways weren't wasted on me. Every time I stepped into my dorm I thought of you. I discovered that I prefer a clean room. I kept trying to think of some way I could get you to visit me on weekends so you could put everything back in order, do my laundry, scrub the toilet and the shower— just a few little things. But since you didn't visit me, I ended up cleaning the place myself." He grinned widely. "Are you proud of me?"

"I'll believe you when I see our room after you've been here this weekend."

"Hey, I don't intend to clean up after myself as long as you're still hanging around. I plan to have breakfast in bed. And if you'd shine my shoes for Sunday and lay my clothes out, I'd appreciate it. I understand that missionaries in Mexico have maids. I'd like to practice up."

Without warning, he tore the pillow from behind his head and flung it at me, hitting me full in the face. "That'll teach you to give me a sorry welcome," he growled, bounding from the bed. "Where's the red carpet? I figured the poplar tree would have a thousand yellow ribbons hanging on it." He had me down on the floor and was pounding playfully on my arm and slapping me on the head. "All you say when I get home is, 'Don't mess up my precious room.' You're lucky I didn't dump your drawers in the middle of the floor."

We wrestled for a moment, then I sensed an advantage and began to twist and wiggle from his grasp. Brad quickly released me and pushed away. "All right," he cautioned, holding up his hands and pretending concern. "You know Mom doesn't like us wrestling up here. You broke a chair the last time. The last thing I want is for you to run whining to Mom."

"You're always quick to start a fight," I accused, "but the first one to tuck tail and run. And you're the one who broke the chair."

"Keep away from me. Who wants his kid brother beating him up?" Panting slightly, he grinned and held out his hand to me. "It's good to see you, Chris." He punched at me when I reached for his hand. "Even if you did forget the yellow ribbons."

"Maybe you should have shown up last night when you were supposed to. Tiffany and I waited up for you." I took his hand and shook it. "Till almost midnight. We had ice cream, cookies, and milk for you. When you didn't show, we ate everything ourselves—and didn't feel a bit guilty. Since we still had a half day of school this morning, we gave up and went to bed."

He ran his fingers through his hair. "The crew hit a water line right before quitting time. Some of the other guys had places to go, but I volunteered to stay. It was after eight before everything was squared away. And believe it or not, I've got to be back on the job Monday morning." He rubbed his forefinger and thumb together. "Besides, I need the money. The overtime helps." He laughed and glanced around the room. "Dang, it's hard to believe that I'll be leaving here." He paused and closed his eyes. "Mexico!" he said slowly with unabashed enthusiasm. "There were a couple of guys on my crew from Sonora, Mexico. They were always speaking Spanish, and I kept thinking, 'In a while I'll be able to understand everything these guys are saying.' One of them lived in Mazatlán while he was growing up. That's in my mission." He smiled and stared at the floor. "Sometimes I wonder if I'm ever going to make it to Mexico."

"You're practically there."

He shrugged. "Sometimes I feel that I'll bust wide open if I don't get down there right now." He smiled. "Your call will be here before you know it."

I straightened the chair and looked around the room where Brad's things were stacked. "I want to go to Russia or Africa, or maybe they'll open up China."

"When that call comes," he said, shaking his head, "it won't matter." He smiled. "Hey, Mom said you're actually going to graduate tonight," he burst out, shoving me and wagging his head, feigning disbelief. "They were probably glad to boot you out, even if it meant giving you a diploma in the process."

I chuckled. "You're not going to rile me." I cleared my throat. "Do you mind if I brag?"

He rolled his eyes. "Will it take long or can you give me the abridged version?"

"Forget it," I muttered, turning away to hide my embarrassed smile. "Just forget it."

"I'm just messing with your brain. Go ahead and brag. I'll put up with it this time." His eyes twinkled in playful torment. "But you won't tell me the same old stuff, will you?"

"Forget you," I grumbled, knowing he was giving me a hard time.

Brad burst out laughing and grabbed my arm. "Hey, man, tell me what's happening."

Jerking my arm free, I struggled to hide my smile. "Get out of my face."

"Mom said your grades were pretty good. You didn't flunk any classes. But, of course, you could sweet-talk the teachers into almost anything. You'd give them that sad-eyed, little doggy look, and they couldn't turn you down." I glared at him. "How'd you end up?" He became serious as he sat on the edge of the bunk and stared at me. His blue eyes reflected a gleeful twinkle that spread from his eyes to the rest of his face.

I coughed, embarrassed. "I ended up with a 3.92—without any arm-twisting or sweet-talk from Mom and Dad."

He whistled softly. "You had all those college prep classes, too. How would it be to be smart? I ended up with an impressive 3.41 GPA. I should have worked harder, like you. But you were always naturally smarter than me. And what was your ACT score, 33?"

"Thirty-one. That's not all that great. Tricia Wilkins and Richie Haroldson both got 32s. Paul McGill got a 34 last year."

"I wish I had a humble 3.92 GPA and a lowly 31 ACT score."

"You didn't need the grades. You had all the glory," I teased. "A three-sport letterman for three years. The Outstanding Athlete Award and the Most Likely to Succeed plaque. You had football and baseball scholarships to choose from."

"Scholarships? I had a chance to play baseball at Cochise College in southern Arizona."

"Snow College has a tough football program," I countered.

"And what did I do all season? I watched the games from the stands with a busted arm." He stared at me. "I'd trade all of that 'glory' for a great big piece of your 3.92 GPA." He shook his head. "I bragged about you all the time, and I'm sure my roommates got sick of hearing about you. They started calling you Saint Christopher." He shrugged. "I didn't care. They were just jealous."

"Aw, don't get mushy with me," I muttered, trying to break the serious mood.

He moved toward the window. There was a far-off look in his eyes as he gazed out the window, and I knew he wasn't seeing anything outside. "You know, Chris, I should have gone on my mission last summer." He turned back to me, pensively probing his molars with his tongue. "The day I broke my arm, I . . ." He hesitated and pushed his hands into his pockets and leaned against the wall. "I knew it was broken even before I felt the rush of pain. I thought to myself, 'Dummy, you should be in the MTC, not here banging heads with these animals.' As they were hauling me inside, I made up my mind that as soon as my arm was better I was going to fill out my papers. I kept changing my mind, though. The mission always got pushed back."

"Your arm was a bummer," I grumbled. "That's probably why things fell apart for you in spring drills."

He shook his head vigorously and smiled. "No, Chris, that quarterback position was mine. Coach talked to me every day, all excited. Shoot, I was excited! We were talking about undefeated seasons, championships, a junior college bowl game. Things were good." He stopped talking and stared at me as though he had explained everything.

"So . . . what made you quit?" I finally asked.

Brad's eyes narrowed slightly. He pursed his lips. "You," he answered simply.

"Aw, get out of my face," I muttered, shaking my head.

"No, I thought of you. Would you wait until there was nothing left to give? Would you wait until things broke down and then give it up and send in your missionary papers?" He shook his head and smiled. "I was willing to give God something—whatever was left over."

Brad took a deep breath and turned back to the window. "The coach knew I'd thought about a mission, but he knew I wanted to play ball. He was counting on that. I was counting on that. During that last practice before I turned in my gear, it was like I couldn't miss. I threw fourteen straight times without a single miss. At the end of the scrimmage I was nineteen out of twenty-one. Do you know what kind of percentage that is?" He didn't wait for me to answer. "And one of those two dropped passes was catchable. I was hot, Chris. I've never been that hot before. Everybody was shaking their heads. Nobody was going to touch me. I just knew it. And then I remembered. Not three hours earlier I'd been telling myself that I should give God my best. I should go on my mission. But when I stared putting up numbers like nineteen out of twenty-one . . ." He whistled and grinned. "I was wavering again."

He stopped talking, and his eyes locked onto mine. "I knew right then, as sure as I'm sitting here, that I could play for Snow, maybe even clinch a winning season or a title. Maybe I'd go on to play for a four-year college." He shook his head. "Maybe not as quarterback, not at 5 foot 10 and 175 pounds."

"You'll fill out on your mission. You can come back at 185 or 190."

Brad shook his head. "I've been charging down this football trail like it was life's superhighway, racing past detours with my eyes closed." He laughed. "I should have hung up my cleats after high school. It was fun while it lasted, but the game's over."

"Give yourself a chance," I blurted out. "You can go places."

"Chris, all these years the one thing I wanted to do was to play ball." He shook his head. "I've started thinking about some of those detours that I've charged past. I'm going to try some of them out. Maybe they're not detours at all. Maybe they're the main roads. Maybe football was the detour." He laughed. "This'll sound crazy, but I'm glad for that busted arm."

"Glad?"

"I'm not saying I would have chosen a busted arm." He rolled his eyes. "I'm not that dumb. But sometimes a thing like that happens, something that you wouldn't have chosen, and that something can be the best thing that ever happened to you."

"Brad, in two years things will be different." I paced the floor. "You don't have to turn in your cleats for good. Just hang them up for a while. They'll still fit in two years."

"I went into the coach's office that afternoon." He went on with his story as though there hadn't been a break. "Right off the coach congratulated me on the afternoon. That's when I dropped the bomb." He took a deep breath and shook his head. "He thought I was kidding at first. He even laughed. Then he saw I was serious. He tried to talk me out of it. He wanted me to think about it some more. I didn't need more time to think. I didn't want more time. I turned my stuff in that afternoon. And when I walked out of there, I knew right then I'd given God the best I had. This time He didn't have to settle for leftovers. I should have done that a year ago."

"Brad, I want you to go on a mission. We've always planned on it. But you don't have to give up football forever to go on a mission."

"*I* do." He was solemn. "And I'm all right with that. It's like I want to sacrifice something, something that means a lot to me. God gave me the talent in the first place. Now I'm giving it back to Him, no strings attached. And you know what, Chris?" He smiled and touched his stomach with his hand. "Inside I feel sure. No more turmoil. No more doubts. I know I'm doing the right thing. A few weeks ago when I was going back and forth, you asked me why I couldn't ever make up my mind. I know now. I wasn't on the right road. Now I am. I'm sure. I've given football up for good!" He smiled wryly and then knit his brow. "I guess what I'm saying is that I'm at peace with myself, more than I've ever been. It's a good feeling. Now I know what you feel like."

Suddenly Brad raised a forefinger. "There is one thing I want to do." A glint of mischief sparkled in his eyes. "Run my marathon."

"Now you *are* talking crazy."

He frowned and shook his head. "I'm running this to prove to *me* that I can. I've been training. Last Saturday I ran eighteen miles, and I'm running the whole marathon before I enter the MTC." He smiled, pointing at me. "And you're running with me."

I gave him the thumbs-down sign.

"Hey, Chris, this will be easy for you."

I laughed.

"I'm dead serious, Chris. I've been training. Even though I put in ten- and eleven-hour days at work, I still run. You got me into the habit."

"What do you mean, *I* got you in the habit? You're the one that dragged me out of bed and talked me into half killing myself."

"So you're in shape, right?"

"I'm in shape. Maybe not your kind of shape, but I get my exercise in." I thought of the hours that Tiffany and I had lugged water to the garden. "And for your information, I still get a few jogs in each week."

"So you've still got your sights on that marathon. That's great, because you're the one that inspired me to run this marathon."

"I hate to break it to you, Brad, but I don't have this marathon on my schedule."

"Now don't weasel out of it. We're going to run just before I leave for the MTC."

"And where is this marathon going to be? In Salt Lake? Ephraim? Where?"

"Chris, we don't need to wait for someone to hold a special event with ribbons and medals and flashing cameras and all of that junk. You can run a marathon anytime, anyplace. All you have to do is go out and run 26.2 miles. This isn't for glory and fame—this is just to prove we can do it. Hey, I'll try to scare you up a ribbon, if that's what you want, but I was just planning on a little quiet, private affair. We'll be the only participants," he rambled on. "We can invite Tiffany to run with us. But she's a sprinter, so a marathon probably doesn't appeal to her like it does to us. But she can come and watch and cheer as we cross the finish line. It'll probably be good to have her there, since somebody should be ready to call the paramedics when we start coughing our guts up."

I listened patiently, trying not to interrupt his rambling. When he finally stopped to catch his breath, I said, "I'm glad you've got it all planned out, Brad. I figure at least fifty percent of the runners will show up and be ready to run on the big day."

"We're going to have one hundred percent participation, Chris."

"Brad," I laughed, shaking my head, "instead of a marathon, why not just lie out in the road and let a few trucks run over you?" I chuckled, but Brad's enthusiasm was contagious. "Of course," I taunted, "I could always beat you in a long race. I could probably cream you in a marathon. But who needs all that pain?" A tremor of uncertainty stirred inside me. I swallowed hard. "A marathon." I said it as though thinking about it for the first time, as though actually contemplating it seriously. I shook my head. "Dang, twenty-six miles. That's torture. You could do stuff like that. You'd just get up one morning and say, 'I guess I'll run a marathon today.' And you'd go out and run a marathon. I hate having a brother that's perfect," I complained, grinning.

"Tell me about it, Saint Christopher. I'm not perfect," Brad smiled ruefully. He clasped his hands in front of him and stared at the floor. "Lately I've wanted you to look up to me," he offered softly. "I don't mean in football or basketball or any ball. I mean in important things. In life."

He was quiet for a long moment. Slowly he rubbed his hands together. We sat there awkwardly for a few minutes, not saying anything, not looking at each other. "What about *your* papers?" he asked after a while.

"Bishop McFadden said I can fill them out anytime now."

"Well, you big dummy," Brad growled at me, starting to slap me about the head, "don't make the same stupid mistake I did. Get an appointment with him. Today. Fill those papers out before something else distracts you. That was my problem."

I laughed, pushed away from his cuffing, and put up my fists. "I've got some time. I don't turn nineteen till the end of July." I jabbed a finger in his direction. "And don't start preaching at me." I stuffed my hands into my back pockets and leaned against the wall. "You're starting to act like Tiffany. She threatens to punch my lights out if I don't get those papers in."

"Good for Tiffany. She knows what you need. By the way, how's she doing?" He didn't wait for me to answer. "I was trying to think of something I could give her as a graduation present. Nothing big or anything. I saw this little stuffed poodle at the store, and I was about to buy that, but somehow I couldn't see Tiffany as the poodle type."

"Why don't you take her out?" I asked unexpectedly.

Brad studied me a moment. "Take her out where?" he asked slowly.

"On a date." I laughed. "It'd give her a thrill."

"Tiffany?"

"No, her mother," I muttered, then I brightened. "She'd like it if you took her out once. But you can't ever tell her that I dropped you the hint. Take my word for it, she'd love it. You know, the big college man returns home, takes the neighbor girl out and gives her a big thrill. You could take her to the dance and the senior all-night party after graduation. She's free tonight. I think she's kept herself open, just in case you ask her."

Brad studied me skeptically with a twisted, sour look on his face.

"Well, it's better than giving her a stupid poodle," I snapped, feeling a little dumb.

Brad grinned. "I'm not sure I want to go on a date with someone I babysat."

"Oh, brother," I moaned, throwing the pillow and hitting him in the head, "you didn't ever babysit Tiffany. Besides, she was more mature when she was born than you were when you were fifteen. Tiffany's a sharp girl. She's smart, athletic, nice to everybody, isn't stuck on herself, and good-looking. You said yourself someone was going to come along and steal her out from under our noses and that we would be big dummies for letting them. Well, this is your chance to snatch her before some other guy does. Ask her out."

"Sounds like you ought to take her," Brad mused.

I rolled my eyes and groaned. "Brad, she doesn't want to go with me. She wants to go with you. I'm all right to hang around with, but you're her dream guy."

"Are we talking about the same Tiffany? Little Tiffany Gibson that's been hanging around here for the last ten years or so?"

"If you weren't almost a missionary, I'd walk over there and rearrange your big, stupid face." I grinned and shook my head. "Forget the date. Go ahead and break her heart. I'll take her to the dance and the senior party. You go out and find another stupid poodle. That will be a great graduation gift."

Brad pretended to ignore me. He got a faraway look in his eyes and said, "I can imagine taking Tiffany out. I'd take her for a walk under a big, bright moon. I'd hold her hand and look into her eyes and get ready to lay a big kiss on her, and then I'd think, 'I used to wipe her nose when she was just a mangy, snotty-nosed kid.'" He shook his head. "She's a little too much like my little sister, except I can't boss her around as much. It'd be mighty tough getting into the mood of the whole date thing. A stuffed poodle might be a bit stupid, but it would be better than trying to start up a romance with Tiffany, don't you think?"

"Personally, I think you're a doofus. You'd be doing her a big favor by not asking her out because her time would be wasted on a goof-brain like you. Buy the stupid poodle. Tiffany probably wouldn't even go out with you, unless she thought you were some charity case."

"So why'd you bring it up?" he asked innocently. "I wasn't looking for a date tonight."

"Forget it!" I grumbled. "She'd rather go with me anyway."

"That's because you never had to wipe her nose." He laughed and threw the pillow back at me. "Besides, there's another reason I can't take her tonight."

I moaned loudly and wagged my head. "Don't even tell me."

"What?"

"You can give up football, but you can't stand to part with that Stacy girl from Tremonton. And I was beginning to believe all that stuff you said about sacrificing football."

"For your information," he came back, his cheeks coloring with embarrassment, "Stacy and I have broken things off. I told her that I didn't want any distractions on my mission. I even told her not to write to me or anything. She was fine with that."

"So, who are you going with tonight?"

He hesitated and cleared his throat, his mouth twisting and twitching. "Stacy," he finally said. "But," he burst out loudly, "I can explain."

"Oh, give me a break," I cut him off, throwing my hands into the air and turning my back to him. "Hold on," I told Brad, turning around and holding up my hand to halt him. "Let me run out to the barn really quick and grab a shovel. It's getting so deep in here that I better shovel some of it out before we both suffocate." I laughed loudly and continued to wag my head. "You've broken things off with Miss Stacy Tremonton because you don't want any distractions going down the homestretch, but you're still going to keep going with her. That's what I call breaking it off. Now that you explain, it sounds very reasonable. I can think of a whole lot of guys that have broken things off with their girlfriends—they just didn't know it. But you make it all sound so logical."

Brad stared at me, a bored look on his face. "Are you finished making a fool of yourself?" he questioned patiently. I smiled mockingly back at him. "I don't know why I'm explaining this to you or even if you're capable of understanding, but I'll do my best to clear things up." He breathed deeply. "Stacy and I have broken things off, but I invited her to go with me tonight. We're going just as friends. It's kind of like our chance to tell each other good-bye. Does that make sense?"

I nodded, trying to appear serious. "Sure. And then next weekend you'll tell her good-bye again. And the week after that, and so forth. And once a week on your mission you'll write this ten-page letter telling her good-bye and that you don't want any distractions. Yeah,

I understand. It makes perfect sense. Thanks for explaining that to me, Brad."

Brad rubbed the back of his neck and pursed his lips. "Now I know what they mean when they say don't throw your pearls before swine." Quickly he threw up his hands to prevent any further response from me. "Hey, Mom said you had a secret." His eyes narrowed and he shook a finger at me. "When did we start keeping secrets?"

"It's not exactly a secret." I grinned. "Do you want to take a ride?"

He glanced at his watch. "What about your graduation?"

"I don't have to be there till seven o'clock. There's plenty of time."

"First, I've got something for you." He nodded toward my top bunk where a package wrapped in light gold foil paper lay on the pillow. I hadn't noticed it until he'd pointed it out. "It's not much. But it's not a stuffed poodle either. I really couldn't see you as a poodle." He fidgeted while he rolled his tongue around in his mouth. "I was hoping to buy you a Porsche or a Corvette." He smiled. "But since you're the practical type, I figured you'd appreciate this more. Besides, what would you do with a Porsche in the middle of Russia or outer Mongolia? And the other missionaries would get jealous." He gave me a quick nudge.

"What is it?" I asked, moving toward the bunk without reaching for the gift. He snatched the present from my pillow and handed it to me. It was heavy and in a box. Carefully I peeled the paper back, trying not to rip it. I set the wrapping paper on Brad's bed and held the plain white box. I lifted the lid and stared down at a set of scriptures—a burgundy, leather-bound quadruple combination. "For me?" I asked, looking up.

"No, for the pope. But he wanted you to autograph it."

"But these are . . ." I gulped, knowing that a set of scriptures like these cost more than fifty dollars; I'd priced some, thinking to buy Brad a set for his mission, but after seeing the price tag, I had settled for a simple copy of *Jesus the Christ*. "These should be yours." I gently brushed my hand over the leather cover and held the scriptures out to Brad. "Why don't you keep them? You're the one leaving on your mission. I can get a set later."

"And what am I supposed to do, scratch your gold-embossed name off the front cover?"

I looked down and saw the bold gold lettering: *Christopher P. Huish.* "Thanks, Brad," I said softly. "I don't know what to say. With a set of scriptures like these, I can't help but be a great missionary." I stared down at the scriptures in my hands and grinned sheepishly, slowly shaking my head. "I guess it's really going to happen, isn't it? I mean, you and me splitting up. It doesn't seem possible." A wave of memories rushed through my mind—years of working, playing, sleeping, eating, and going to school together.

"It was bound to happen," he said, pretending to be indifferent. "But it's probably just as well. I can't have my kid brother tagging along with me all the time. People would think I was weird." He glanced over at me and grinned broadly. "I'm going to miss you, bro," he said sincerely. "I wish you were tagging along."

"Just in case your maid in Mexico doesn't clean up after you?"

He chuckled. "That, too, but it's more than that." He chewed pensively on his lower lip. "Do you remember Rhett Bundy?" he asked unexpectedly. "I don't know why he popped into my head. You were in fourth grade." He laughed. "Remember?"

I smiled wanly. "How could I forget Rhett Bundy and the fight?"

Rhett, a sixth-grade bully, had tormented me for weeks until finally one lunch hour I'd fought him in exasperation. I didn't stand a chance. He was twenty-five pounds heavier and five inches taller. I didn't land a single punch and ended up with my nose bloody and my lip split.

That's when Brad found us surrounded by a circle of cheering peers, hungry to witness a fight. Brad took Rhett on, but he fared worse than I did because he was a scrapper and refused to quit until Rhett had thoroughly thumped him. There we stood, huffing and blubbering and dripping blood down onto our shirt fronts while Rhett gloated over his victory. It wasn't fair. It wasn't right. We were the victims, and we had lost.

I was ready to slink away, but Brad touched my arm and said the unthinkable, and said it loud enough for Rhett to hear: "Maybe one of us can't take him alone, but two of us can take him together." Before Rhett could erase the smirk from his face, we jumped him, and the fight began in earnest. Rhett landed a couple of good blows and Brad and I were soon bawling again, but this time the tears weren't from pain; they were tears of sheer determination.

Rhett went down, smothered under our onslaught of flying fists. He finally surrendered, promising peace. The three of us faced each other again, panting and bleeding and glaring at each other. The three of us were also suspended, and the afternoon after our suspension, Rhett followed us home from school. Not to fight. We were friends, apparently.

"Rhett taught us that we could do anything together," Brad mused. "We'll be in different places, Chris, but we'll still be together." He reached down and took the quadruple combination from my hands and flipped causally through the thin, crisp pages. Closing the book, he cleared his throat and handed the scriptures back to me. "What's the big secret?" He grabbed his shoes, put them on, and started lacing them. "Give me a hint?"

I set the scriptures on my pillow, stepped to the window, pulled the cotton curtains back, and gazed down on the back lawn where Lisa was teaching our puppy, Shag, to fetch a ball. "Remember when we planned to grow watermelons up in the garden?"

"Yeah, I remember," he groaned. "And when we finally wised up, we decided that growing watermelons up here was about as stupid as growing pineapples on the North Pole."

I turned back to him, struggling to contain my enthusiasm. Brad studied me. Gradually his eyes narrowed. "You didn't."

"I figure the first melons will ripen the end of July, maybe the first of August," I gushed. "We seeded the hotbeds in April."

"Hotbeds? You mean, like we'd planned?"

I nodded. "We used space heaters and fans and . . ." I grinned. "You wouldn't believe how they grew. Our biggest worry was that the plants would be so big that we'd never get the vines untangled enough to get them in the ground. Then, once we got them transplanted, we had to haul water in barrels in the back of the truck to keep the plants from dying, because our first irrigation turn isn't till tomorrow evening. We had a heck of a time cleaning out the ditch down to the garden. I almost rolled the tractor twice." I shook my head and took a deep breath.

"We? Who's this *we* you keep talking about?"

"It was really Tiffany's idea. She's the one who pushed it at first. I'd never have made it without her. We're figuring on twelve hundred melons at . . . three, four, maybe five dollars a melon. These will be big melons. And fresh. People coming up to the reservoir in the summer are going to jump at the chance to buy a good melon. We'll sell them easy. Four thousand dollars maybe, give or take a few hundred." I grinned. "We weren't sure it was going to work, so we kept it a secret."

"It could still freeze," he warned.

I shook my head. "No way!" I laughed. "Tiffany wouldn't put up with a freeze. She has already decided that the weather is absolutely going to cooperate. Maybe that's why we've had such a mild spring and good rain. It won't freeze." I clenched my fist and pressed it against my stomach. "I feel it here. It's going to work, Brad. I know it. And those watermelons helped me get an A in Professor Hill's botany class. They were my major project. He even came up to see them, and boy, was he impressed."

Brad studied me reflectively without saying anything. Finally he whistled softly. "Let's take that ride, Christopher P." Shaking his head, he added, "Maybe a guy *can* grow pineapples on the North Pole. All he needs is you with your wild imagination and your smokin' 3.92 GPA."

CHAPTER TEN

I tossed Brad the keys as we trotted out to the Chevy. The truck's doors whined a protest as we opened them. "We better pick up Tiffany," Brad suggested, sliding onto the seat and slamming the door. "If we don't at least invite her," he joked, "she'll bawl that we left her out of something."

We left the truck running and marched up Tiffany's front walk. The door opened before we even knocked. "So the big college man has returned," Tiffany teased, stepping through the doorway, putting her arms around Brad's neck and giving him a hug

"She doesn't ever greet me like that when I come over," I teased. Tiffany pushed away from Brad and grabbed for me. "I wasn't complaining," I said, holding up my hands and backing away, but she caught me, pulled me toward her, and hugged me too.

Tiffany was wearing white-denim knee shorts and a blue pullover cotton knit shirt. Her feet were bare. Her hair was wet, and her face was makeup-free, but her wide, contagious smile flashed freely.

"We're taking you for a ride," Brad announced. "Come peaceably without a big hassle."

"Brad's been complaining about all the times he's had to babysit you and wipe your nose. He said he didn't want you pitching a royal fit because we had left you behind," I teased.

Tiffany put on a look of fake sternness and put her hands on her hips. "Bradley Huish, when did you ever babysit me? And you sure didn't ever wipe my nose."

Brad blushed deeply. "Chris wasn't supposed to tell you that. I was just kidding. Are you coming or are you going to stand here and sulk?"

Tiffany looked from Brad to me. She glanced at her wrist, but her watch was missing. "I've still got a million things to do. I just got out of the shower."

Brad shrugged indifferently. "Since this is a special occasion," he said, "we won't make you run behind the truck like usual. You can ride in the back if you'll keep your head down so people won't know you're tagging along. Of course, you'll still have to open all the gates, and if we get stuck, you'll need to get out and push." Tiffany twisted her mouth into an angry pout, and her eyes narrowed threateningly, but he continued, "Do you want your shoes or do we haul you to the truck the way you are? We don't have time to deal with your feminine emotional yo-yo."

Turning to me, she remarked, "After a year of college, most people grow up and acquire a little grace and charm." She jerked a thumb in Brad's direction. "What happened to him?" I laughed and shook my head.

"Nothing's changed with her," Brad lamented lightly. "Still bossy and trying to call all the shots."

A moment later Tiffany walked to the truck carrying her sandals and wearing her Raiders cap over her wet hair. Brad helped her in on the driver's side so she could sit between us.

The dirt road leading to the garden was a dual-wheel path that crossed a meadow and snaked through tall brush, weeds, and grass to rolling hills hiding the garden. Brad parked the truck on an old wooden-plank bridge that crossed the irrigation canal. Because the trail leading from the bridge to the garden was narrow and cramped between two round ridges, it was tough maneuvering a vehicle down it. Since we didn't need the truck in the garden, we left it at the bridge.

Just before the trail leveled out at the bottom of the hill, it took a forty-five-degree turn and then opened up on a miniature two-acre valley. Until a person came around that last turn, the garden was hidden from view. As soon as we came around the turn, Brad stared out across the garden. For a moment he didn't say anything, then slowly he muttered, "I don't believe it."

There were eighteen carefully measured rows of watermelon, forty hills per row. The melon vines had started to spread, each clump of vines already measuring a yard or so in diameter. Brad walked toward the first row. He reached down and lifted some of the vines. "They even have a few blossoms."

"Clarence Walker's going to bring some of his beehives up the first of next week," I explained, fighting down my excitement.

"You're a genius, Chris. You two will be rich."

"Actually, they're yours, too," I said.

He shook his head. "I haven't done anything, but I wish I had. I could use the cash."

Becoming serious, I gazed out over the dull-green watermelon vines rapidly covering the garden's black soil. "We used to dream about striking it rich. There were going to be lines of cars in front of our place, people just waiting for one of our famous melons."

Brad motioned toward the garden with outstretched arms. "You pulled it off."

"Tiffany wanted this for our missions. These are mission melons," I explained.

Brad looked at me, then at Tiffany. "I don't get it."

"You haven't had a lot of time to save up for your mission, so we figured the watermelons would help," Tiffany explained. "The money is for both you and Chris."

"Tiffany's done more than her share of the work," I said to Brad. "She helped with the hotbeds. She was here when we transplanted. The last two weeks we've hauled water out here in barrels." I smiled over at her while she blushed slightly.

"And what do you get out of it, Tiffany?" Brad wanted to know.

Tiffany's cheeks turned a deeper pink, and she looked away, surveying the garden. "I guess I get the satisfaction of helping a couple of friends."

"That doesn't sound like too much," Brad remarked, keeping his eyes on Tiffany.

She shrugged and turned back to him. "Well, that's what I wanted to do. And since you're no longer my babysitter, I figured I didn't need your permission to do it."

Brad laughed. "I deserved that." He shook his head, pushed his hands into his pockets, and walked down the rows, leaving Tiffany and me standing at the top of the garden.

"Just seeing his face is worth all the work and sweat and dirt and mud," Tiffany whispered. She leaned her shoulder against mine and laughed softly. "A month or so from now he'll be gone. I already miss him." She bent over, picked up a dirt clod, and tossed it.

"You say your first irrigation turn is tomorrow?" Brad asked as he ambled back to us.

"At seven o'clock in the evening. We would've gotten the water earlier, but Dan Arney, the water master, didn't have this piece on the regular schedule because it's been so long since anybody has used it for anything. Dan had to do some rearranging to squeeze us in."

Brad looked around. "The head ditches aren't dug. You need furrows down the rows."

"He shows up one time," Tiffany kidded, taking my arm and nodding toward Brad, "and he thinks he's the farmer. Do you suppose he figured we were just going to flood the whole garden without getting the ditches ready?"

Brad smiled sheepishly, flipping Tiffany's hair and looking at his watch. "We better get the princess back before she panics."

"You're going, aren't you?" Tiffany asked him hopefully. "To commencement, I mean."

"I don't know if I'm up to sitting through a long, dry commencement exercise."

Shrugging, Tiffany mused, "It isn't every day that you get to see Chris and me march across the stage in long, flowing red-and-white robes and balancing funny hats on our heads. I might even do a cartwheel or two across the stage."

"I have to sit through two hours of boring speeches to see you two walk a few feet? Even with a good cartwheel thrown in, that's quite a sacrifice."

Tiffany looked over at me with an expression of exasperation. "Tell him to stay home."

Brad burst out laughing. "I'm going. I'm more excited about tonight than you two combined. Just don't get embarrassed when I stand up on my chair and cheer as you snatch your diplomas. They'll probably send security to throw me out for disturbing the peace."

After dropping Tiffany off at her place, Brad commented, "Tiffany's all right." He whistled softly. "Maybe I shouldn't have invited Stacy to go with me tonight."

I looked at Brad, a questioning look on my face. He just shrugged noncommittally. We spent the rest of the ride home in silence.

* * *

Tiffany greeted me when I reached the school that evening. "I didn't think you were going to make it. I was getting nervous, and you're the only one who can calm me down." Her flat mortar-board cap was perched on top of her head and pinned down, slightly squashing her hair. She stood straight and pompous in her white, silky graduation robe. "It's really happening, Chris." Nervously she pressed her lips together, took my hand, and squeezed it between both of hers. She seemed genuinely glad to see me. We joked and exchanged light, anxious chatter as we lined up, while Mr. Holden, the principal, gave last-minute instructions, reminding us of the importance of this auspicious occasion and challenging us to be dignified.

The evening was a whirlwind of activity as we sat through commencement exercises. After receiving our diplomas, we graduates whooped it up on the football field while our parents and families came down to congratulate us, take group pictures, and reminisce about the past years of our high-school experience.

"Hey, you really have started keeping secrets from me." Brad accused as he came up with Stacy, shook my hand, and gave me a long, tight hug. "You didn't say anything about a scholarship."

"I didn't know until they announced it," I said, my cheeks coloring. "But tonight wasn't anything like your graduation last year." I grinned.

"You're right," Brad came back seriously. "Your scholarship means something." He grabbed me again and squeezed me. "Dang, I'm proud of you."

Tiffany walked over to us, and Brad gave her a hug and then stepped back and looked her up and down. "You're getting all grown-up, Tiffany." He turned to me and pretended to whisper. "I guess there won't be any more sleepovers in the backyard with Tiffany. And I don't think she needs a babysitter anymore. Her mom gave her a handkerchief before the ceremonies, so I think she can take care of her own nose now."

Tiffany lightly slapped him. "Your joke is getting a little old, Brad."

"Hey, Stacy," Brad said, turning to his date. "This is Tiffany Gibson." He turned back to Tiffany and me. "She knows all about you."

Stacy laughed. "All he talks about is all the crazy things the three of you used to do. He talks about it so much that it feels like I was there."

We continued with small talk, then Stacy and Brad excused themselves and wandered off. "They look nice together," Tiffany remarked as she watched them go.

"Are you jealous?" I asked, nudging her with my elbow.

She thought a moment, pursing her lips. "I stopped being jealous a long time ago," she said, smiling faintly. Impetuously, she reached out and slipped her arm through mine. "Why would I be jealous?" she said in a deep, husky voice. "I get his younger brother." She cleared her throat and straightened up. "Of course, the younger brother still hasn't asked me to go with him to the dance and party tonight." She tossed her head, flipping her hair over her shoulders. "But I'm patient," she added. "He's usually late, but he always gets around to it."

"I didn't know you wanted to go with me," I stammered, genuinely surprised. "I was waiting for Brad to make your day. I was—"

"Are *you* going to ask *me*," she said, heaving a sigh, "or do *I* have to ask you? This is really embarrassing, Chris. I hate asking guys out."

Leaning toward her, I asked boldly, "Tiffany, would you spend the night with me?"

In mock astonishment she jerked her arm from mine and jumped back. "Now you're getting too fresh. What do you mean, 'spend the night with you?'"

Although I knew she was joking, her words and reaction startled me, and my face flushed a deep red—almost purple. "It's an all-night dance and party, Tiffany. Will you go with me?"

She relaxed ostensibly, winked, and took my arm again. "I'd love to. And thanks for not making me ask you. Although I did have to hint."

Tiffany and I stayed together throughout the entire dance; then we went to the senior all-night party, although we ended up leaving early. It was almost four o'clock in the morning when we groggily drove over the mountain to Eden, finally willing to abandon the waning graduation activities.

As I helped her out of the car, she took my hand and held it. Although it was still dark, there were already faint traces of morning sun glimmering in the eastern sky. The air was a bit chilly, so Tiffany pushed up close to me and shivered. "I don't want it to end," she said ruefully.

"School?"

"Everything."

"I guess it's too late to do anything about that," I joked.

"No, it's not," she argued. "We can still prolong things. Let's go for a walk."

"A walk?" I squinted down at my watch. "Do you know how late it is?"

She didn't answer. Instead, she tightened her hold on my hand and began pulling me after her. "I want to stroll in the city park." Then she added, "Barefoot." I followed her.

As soon as we reached the park, she kicked off her shoes and brushed her bare feet through the shaggy grass. Neither one of us spoke as we walked hand in hand. All evening I had been feeling something strangely unfamiliar stir inside me as I had been with Tiffany. And as the night progressed, I was startled to realize that these feelings weren't exactly new. They were just feelings that I had ignored or pushed into the back of my mind. But I realized that I liked Tiffany, not just as a family friend or the neighbor across Eden. I felt something more intense, more deep than friendship. I found myself wanting to hold her and never let her slip away from me. What I found so utterly baffling is that it had taken me so long to actually realize what was going on inside me. I was glad that she had wanted to go on this walk because I feared that once this evening was over, everything would somehow slip back to the way it had always been, and I didn't want that to happen. Ever.

"So it's the big bad world for both of us now," she remarked softly. "What are you going to do? Besides take care of your watermelon patch."

"Starting Monday, Wilson Tanner wants me to work for him hanging drywall."

"Sounds fun." Her laugh was soft and musical.

"Actually, it's a killer, but I'll make good money and get lots of overtime. Do you still plan to start working at Gilroy's?"

"A week from Monday." Suddenly she dropped down on the grass and pulled me down next to her. She still kept my hand. "I think I could just crash here on the grass and go to sleep." She yawned, and a lone car drove slowly down the street on the north side of the park. "Somebody will see us out here at this time of the morning and they'll stir up a regular scandal. Are you ready to be scandalized? We could be the hot summer gossip in Eden." She giggled, pushing up from the ground and pulling me up after her. "I'm hyper, Chris. I can't settle down." She laughed, and the sound seemed to carry across the park and echo throughout the whole town. Suddenly, she dropped my hand and charged recklessly across the park to where she had left her shoes a few minutes earlier.

I was tempted to chase after her, but instead I strolled casually behind until I caught up to her. She was sitting on the grass, her shoes on her feet. "I hate to tell you this, Chris, but I think my dad's out here someplace looking for me. You better get me home before he catches you. He'll want to know why you didn't get me home sooner."

"It was your idea for a walk," I reminded her, holding my hand out to pull her up. She held up both her hands, and I took them and pulled her to her feet. Intentionally she fell against me, causing me to stagger backward, then she quickly jerked away and skipped toward home, pulling me along behind her.

When we reached the Gibsons' house, we strolled up the front walk and stopped in the dim yellow light on the front steps. "This night isn't what I had expected," she said, looking at me. "I imagined it was going to be different."

"In what way?"

"In lots of ways."

"Has it been better or worse?"

She pursed her lips and cocked her head to one side, her eyes narrowing slightly. "Better. Definitely better." She seemed to be studying me quite intently.

Her steady gaze made me feel a bit nervous and awkward. "Well, I guess this is how twelve years of school end," I managed inanely. I took her hand again.

She looked down at her hand in mine as we stood face-to-face. "So this is how it all ends, with a shake of the hand?" Tiffany asked dramatically, putting her free hand to her forehead and pretending to half faint. "And I was expecting so much more. Especially on graduation night." She looked around. "Or shall I say graduation morning?"

I smiled, and then exhibiting a boldness that rarely showed itself, but one that had been gradually building inside me all evening, I dropped her hand, put my hands on her waist, pulled her toward me, and kissed her on the lips, taking her entirely by surprise. I suppose I even surprised myself.

For a moment she just stood there with her eyes wide and her mouth partially open. "Chris!" she finally gasped, taking a deep, gulping breath.

I shrugged with embarrassment. "Is that a better ending?" She managed a breathless smile and touched her lips with her fingertips. I added, "We graduate only once. That's something to remember me by."

She smiled. "I'll remember that. I promise." After a suspicious look my way, she stifled a yawn with the back of her hand and giggled. "That wasn't because of your kiss," she explained teasingly, and jabbed me with her finger.

"I wondered," I said, trying to sound playful rather than nervous, fidgeting from one foot to the other. "I could try again," I offered hopefully. "I don't want my only kiss to be a yawner."

She smiled and bit down on her lower lip in a coquettish way. I wanted to hold her and kiss her once more. I was about to reach for her hand again when she said quietly, "Thank you, Chris. It was a great way to end twelve years." Before I could say anything else, she slipped away from me and disappeared into the house.

CHAPTER ELEVEN

O ur house was quiet as I opened my eyes and looked around
the bedroom. The sun sent bars of yellow light piercing
through the cotton curtains at the window. I peeked over the
edge of the bunk. Brad's bed was made. I glanced at the alarm clock on
the desk—12:30 P.M. Crashing back on my pillow, I moaned, rubbed
my eyes, and stretched.

As I tumbled out of bed and steadied myself on the floor, I spotted
a sheet of lined yellow notebook paper, folded several times, taped to
the mirror. I pulled it off and slowly unfolded it. *THIS IS THE MARA-
THON COURSE,* Brad had written in block letters. In smaller letters he
had added, *I measured it this morning. Get serious about your training,
Chris. June 30th is the big day. That's the Saturday before I enter the
MTC. Remember, no trophies, ribbons, or medals—just private, personal
glory!* He had drawn two racing stick figures with goofy smiles on
their balloon-shaped heads.

I smiled, studying the pencil-drawn map on the bottom of the page.
The course started in Eden, looped the reservoir and Huntsville, jogged
up the road toward the monastery, and then back through Eden and
Liberty, ending in North Fork Park at the far north end of the valley.

"He's crazy," I muttered. "Persistent, but still crazy. And I'm crazier
if I run with him." I folded the note and tossed it on the top of the
dresser. "I'll pass up the glory, Brad."

I tromped downstairs. "Is that you, Chris?" Mom called from the
laundry room.

"I think so," I mumbled drowsily, making my way to the kitchen.
"Where is everybody?"

Mom came into the kitchen and tousled my hair. "I didn't think you were ever going to roll out of that bunk. Do you want breakfast, lunch, or an early dinner? At this time of day, you can take your pick. We had cold chicken sandwiches for lunch."

"A sandwich sounds fine. Where's Brad?"

"He's been out at the garden today. He took the old tractor this afternoon. Your dad offered to let him take the new one, but Brad said he felt more comfortable on the old one."

I scratched the back of my head and closed my eyes. "I hope he doesn't dump it in the ditch going down that narrow lane."

Mom laughed. "He'll do fine," she replied as she took out a loaf of bread. "The radio said a cold front's moving in," she remarked worriedly. "Do you think your watermelons will be all right?"

"We've survived a couple of cold nights. Things don't look all that bad out there."

"It is cooler today."

"They'll be fine, Mom. Have some faith," I answered.

After wolfing down two sandwiches and drinking three glasses of milk, I drove the Chevy to the garden and parked it at the canal. I walked from there to the garden. Brad was in the middle of the melon patch on the tractor.

"About time you showed up."

I turned. Tiffany, dressed in a pair of denim jeans, a baggy, long-sleeved cotton shirt, boots, and her Raiders cap, sat at the top of the field under a squatty juniper tree. "How long have you been here?" I questioned sheepishly, walking over to where she sat.

"Longer than you. We're almost finished. As usual, you show up when the work's done."

I dropped down beside her. "Once I hit the sack, I died. When did you get up?"

She shook her head. "I can't sleep when I know there's work to do," she said lightly. "I couldn't let Brad do all this by himself."

Tiffany picked up a dirt clod and tossed it out into the field. Ostentatiously she cleared her throat. "You must have had a wild night last night." She jabbed me with her elbow, pulled off her hat, and studied it. "I always thought you were pretty shy."

"And what's that supposed to mean?" I felt my cheeks color.

"Just an observation. Don't get all defensive on me, Chris." I suspected she was referring to my impetuous, last-minute kiss. She chuckled and looked over at me. "Oh, I guess we'd better change the subject. You're getting all embarrassed."

"I'm not embarrassed," I grumbled jokingly, refusing to look in her direction.

"There's a big multistake dance in Ogden tonight," she stated casually, looking away. "But you're probably not up to two wild nights in a row."

I looked over at her. She was trying not to smile, but her blue eyes teased as she looked out across the field.

"I just might go to that dance," I declared, studying the garden.

"Are you taking somebody?" Before I could answer, she went on, "Because if you do, you'd have to get them in before five thirty Sunday morning. Nice girls don't like to stay out that late." She pressed the back of her hand to her mouth and laughed.

"You're really on one today, aren't you?" I said wryly. "Are you going to the dance?"

"Nobody's asked me. And I don't go around asking guys, especially wild ones. You know, the ones that . . ." she paused, ". . . catch you off guard."

"Aren't you in a dramatic mood today," I responded dryly.

Tiffany gave me a quick, prankish shove. "Chris, you know that I'm in love with you and that I'm just messing around."

"I thought you were in love with Brad," I returned.

She put her finger to her chin, thought for a moment, and shrugged. "Oh, I'd forgotten about that." She sighed heavily. "You still haven't answered my question about the dance."

Fighting back a grin, I answered, "Actually, I know this pretty wild girl that stays out really late and . . ."

"Don't go any further," she cut me off with pretended formality. "I can't bear to hear about your wild women."

For a few minutes we watched Brad drive the tractor. "He's had fun today," Tiffany remarked, more serious now. "It surprised him to realize how much he's missed the farm."

"Brad? Miss the farm?" I said doubtfully. "He's got bigger things to do than farm."

"Oh, I'm not so sure," Tiffany said slowly. "We were weeding a while ago, and he leaned on his hoe, looked out across the garden, and said, 'I used to dread hoeing anything, but I'm getting a bang out of this.'" She smiled. "He was having fun, hacking weeds and sweating."

"Hacking weeds and sweating can get old really fast. He can enjoy it one Saturday when he knows Monday he'll be away from here on a construction crew making big bucks." I was quiet a moment and then asked hesitantly, "Are you sure you want to put all this work into this garden and then turn around and hand the profits to Brad?"

"That's the fun of the whole thing, giving all of it away for a mission." She laughed and pulled her legs up in front of her, wrapped her arms around them, and rested her chin on her knees. "It's too bad that Brad won't be able to see the garden when it's covered with ripe watermelons. He'd love that." She nudged me with her knee.

When Brad pulled closer to us, he yelled to me, "Hey, who kissed the prince?"

I turned to Tiffany, giving her an accusatory glare. She held up her hand and whispered, "I didn't say a word. I'm not like that." She poked me with a finger and snickered, "It's your guilty conscience."

Brad surveyed the melon patch. "When I catch the plane for Mexico, I want you to bring me a great big melon to the airport. We'll sit down in the middle of the terminal and bust that baby open and stuff ourselves, spitting seeds everywhere." He laughed.

I picked up a dirt clod and tossed it at him. "First we better worry about getting the water down those furrows this evening or we won't have anything." I pushed up from the ground and dusted off my pants. "The head ditches aren't ready, and the north side still needs furrowing."

"A regular slave driver!" he protested, winking at Tiffany. "It was easier when it was just the two of us out here and he was back at the house sleeping like the pampered prince."

For the rest of the afternoon the three of us worked to finish furrowing the remainder of the garden, weeding and fixing the head ditches across the top of the patch and getting things ready for our irrigation turn. It was like old times, the three of us laughing, bragging, teasing, tossing dirt clods at each other, and threatening to toss each other into the ditch when we turned the water on.

"Now that I've done most of the work," Tiffany finally sighed a little after six thirty, "do you two think you can water this little patch of ground by yourselves?" She wiped her brow with her shirtsleeve. "I told Mom I'd be home by six. I'm already late."

"Don't tell me you're going to miss our first irrigation turn," I objected cheerfully.

Putting her hands on her hips, she pensively surveyed the garden. "Well, as much as I hate to, I guess you and big brother will have to do it yourselves. There will be other irrigation turns for me. Unless, of course, you two do something stupid, flood the whole place and wash all the plants away. I mean," she said sardonically, "you can do this on your own, can't you?"

"Aren't you glad we have only one mother?" Brad grinned at me. "I know Tiffany really wants to play the mother, but she doesn't have the hang of it. There's something about her style that's just a little . . ." He pondered, pressing his lips together while he kicked at the dirt.

"Annoying?" I helped him out.

"Annoying isn't quite strong enough, but it'll do. Has she been like this the whole time?"

"Mostly." Brad and I turned our backs to Tiffany, ignoring her. "Actually," I continued, "if she'd worked as hard as she claims, we could have put in about ten or twenty acres of melons. The main reason I let her in on this project is that I'm trying to build her self-esteem, make her feel like she's really doing something. It's something I promised her mother I'd do for her."

"So this whole melon patch is really a personal improvement project for Tiffany," Brad replied.

Suddenly we were pelted by a barrage of dirt clods. We didn't even have time to defend ourselves, so, ducking our heads and holding our hands and arms up to protect us from the onslaught, Brad and I charged into the garden to escape. "Had enough?" she shouted after us.

Laughing, we turned to face her. "Hey, Tiffany," Brad joked, "we didn't know you were still here. We thought you'd left."

She picked up another dirt clod, about half the size of her fist, and chucked it at him. "You better watch out," she warned, "because if I find a good throwing rock, I'm going to bounce it off your heads. Then you'll see what my self-esteem is like."

Holding up our hands, we surrendered peacefully and returned to the top of the garden. "You're all right, Tiffany," Brad teased. "In fact, I was getting ready to give you a thrill and ask you out." He flashed his engaging grin and winked at me. "Is there anything going on tonight?"

Tiffany gave him a look of mild disgust. "There's a dance, but I'm very selective. What makes you think I'd be thrilled to go with an old farmer like you?"

"Because I'm the man. I've got charm. I'm a real hunk. I'm debonair. I'm everything someone like you is looking for. Shall I go on?"

"Just out of curiosity, is humility one of your manly traits?"

Brad's smile broadened. "Humility?" he asked, his brow wrinkling. "I'm not sure that humility is one of the traits I've worked on lately."

"Really? What a shock!"

"So you'll go with me? Unless you've accepted someone else's invitation."

All of this talk of the dance caught me off guard. Tiffany smiled at Brad. "No one has actually asked me," she admitted.

"Then I'm asking—before somebody beats me to it. I'll pick you up at nine o'clock." Brad turned to me and gave me a quick push on the shoulder. "Maybe Chris'll scare up a date and we'll double."

"I'm not going," I interjected quickly, unable to keep the cool snap from my tone.

"So it's just the two of us." Brad went on, oblivious to my mood change. "Is it a date?" he pressed. His tanned, perspiring face crinkled in a teasing grin.

"How can I resist such an invitation?" Tiffany answered, blushing and looking down at the ground. "I guess I'll be waiting for the thrill of my life." She snorted, turned, and headed up the trail while Brad watched her disappear.

Only moments before we had been joking. All of that had changed with Brad's unexpected invitation to Tiffany. I hadn't actually asked her to go with me; we had only joked, but I had assumed that in my teasing was an invitation to the dance. The last person I expected to interfere with my unspoken plans was Brad. After all, he hadn't exhibited any interest in Tiffany the previous afternoon when I had tried to encourage him. But now I was sure I felt different about Tiffany, and I didn't want Tiffany going with Brad. I found myself perplexed by a turmoil of emotions. I resented Brad for intruding so brazenly, even if it was innocently, and I was hurt that Tiffany had accepted Brad's invitation so readily.

"Why don't you double with us?" Brad asked, turning back to me.

"I've got the garden to think about," I muttered, walking away.

"But we'll be finished here before nine o'clock."

"I've got the garden on my mind, not some dance." I knew if Brad even suspected that I liked Tiffany, he would joke and let me take her, but that wasn't how I wanted Tiffany. And, sadly, I wasn't sure what Tiffany wanted.

Brad started gathering up the hoes and the shovels. "Tiffany's grown up, Chris. I've watched her today. I've thought of Stacy, too. And other girls." He paused and pondered. "Tiffany's got them all beat." He laughed as he leaned the shovels and hoes against the little juniper tree. "A lot of good it does me, though. I'm leaving. Somebody else will grab her. Here we've practically raised her, shown her the ropes, turned her into a hot item, and when we're all finished, somebody else gets her. It's not fair. We're being robbed."

I didn't respond to his monologue, but my silence must have been revealing because Brad asked me bluntly, though in good humor, "What's treading on your nerves?"

"Let's get the tractor out of the field before the water comes." I couldn't look at him because I knew he could read the emotions on my face.

"Something's eating you," Brad accused, still cheerful. "All of a sudden you've got your shorts in a knot. What's happening, man?"

The muscles along my jaw tightened. I was as angry with myself for becoming as upset as I was with Brad for asking Tiffany out. "Let's just get the garden ready for irrigation," I growled.

Slowly he stuffed his hands in his pockets. "Chris, something's rubbed you the wrong way." Stubborn, I didn't answer. Out of the corner of my eye I watched him study me inquiringly. "Does it have anything to do with Tiffany?"

"Just leave it alone, Brad," I snapped.

"Did you ask her?"

"No!" I snapped again.

"But you were going to ask her?" he asked, genuinely surprised.

"Who took her last night when you weren't interested?" I returned, unable to control the edge to my voice. I finally faced him, pressing my lips together to hide my anger.

Brad's smile drooped from his face. "Hey, I wasn't trying to cut in on you. You're the one that told me to ask her out." He shrugged. "I thought that's what you wanted me to do."

"You've never shown any interest in her. You've always wanted somebody better than Tiffany." The words spilled out in a rush. "I took her to homecoming because you couldn't bother. You asked her out, then stood her up."

"I cleared all of that up," he said, seemingly stunned by my onslaught of words.

"How? By telling her at the last minute you weren't going with her? She'd already turned two guys down, expecting you to take her. Then when she needed a date, she couldn't go back to them. She came to me, but she wanted to go with you." I didn't know if my gush of words made sense, and until right then, I didn't realize that I had harbored such harsh resentment.

"Chris, I didn't know any of this."

"Yeah," I muttered, "you were too busy with yourself." I turned away and stared out across the garden so I wouldn't have to look at Brad. I swallowed hard, shocked and a bit remorseful that I had allowed my anger to flare up so blatantly, especially today.

For a moment neither of us said anything. Brad dropped down on his haunches, grabbed a handful of dirt, and let it sift through his fingers. "Look, Chris," he said sympathetically, "I asked Tiffany because you suggested it yesterday." He stood up and dusted his hand off on his pant leg. "You can take her tonight. I'm okay with that."

"Sure," I murmured. "You'll just call her up and say, 'Hey, Chris wants to go with you more than I do, so go with him.' That's a great plan. She wants to go with you," I ended bitterly.

Brad shook his head and exhaled loudly. "Well, we can figure this out later. Now we better get that water down here before our turn is up. I'll drive the tractor up the hill."

"I'll get it," I countered, starting for the tractor, which was parked twenty feet away.

Brad stepped ahead of me and reached the tractor first. "Hey, I've pampered this old crate of bolts all afternoon. I'll drive her out of here."

"I ought to drive the tractor," I came back. "It's tough getting it up that hill."

"I got it down here," he replied, his cheery disposition returning. "I've driven it all day, and I haven't busted anything. I'll manage."

I don't know why I was so stubborn—Brad had apologized—but for some reason I tried to move around Brad so I could climb up onto the tractor. "This garden is my project."

Brad quickly pulled himself onto the tractor seat. Grinning down at me, he answered, "Hey, I'm not taking your project away, but I can drive the tractor up the hill. Grab the shovels and hoes and hop on the back. You better leave one shovel here. We'll need it for irrigation." He shook a finger at me. "But if you're going to ride with me, I don't want any backseat driving," he joked.

"I'll walk," I muttered, turning away and starting to gather up the shovels and hoes. "But it's tough going up that trail," I flung at him caustically. "Especially around the bend."

"Chris, I was driving this tractor a long time before you ever took it." He laughed. "I'm the one that showed you how to drive it. Remember? A year at college didn't make me forget everything. I promise I won't get bucked off." He continued to grin as he leaned his forearms on the steering wheel.

"The last thing I need is to spend the night pulling that tractor out of a hole," I grumbled, starting toward the trail, my arms loaded with shovels and hoes. I wanted him to bite back. I wanted to ruffle and frustrate him, but he seemed undaunted, unwilling to be drawn into a verbal skirmish with me. I glanced toward the bottom of the field. "Is that your jacket down there?" I accused, nodding with my head. "Are you going to just leave it there?"

"Thanks. I'll get it," he called, jumping down from the tractor. "When you get up the hill, turn the water on." I kept walking, not acknowledging his last words. "Hey, Chris," he called again, his voice conciliatory, "if you really want to drive this tractor up the hill, take it. Just leave the shovels and hoes there and I'll haul them up after I grab my jacket."

Stubbornly ignoring his offer, I kept walking. By the time I reached the truck, parked on the plank bridge spanning the irrigation canal, I heard the distant growl of the tractor engine starting up the incline.

Still battling my smoldering anger, I squatted next to the canal, listening to the soft, gentle flow of the water as it moved past. I snatched a tuft of grass, tossed it into the stream, and watched it break up into individual blades and float away. To my left a snake slipped into the current, bringing me out of my silent pondering. I studied it for a moment and then teased it with a stick. It dodged one way, then back the other as I kept the stick in front of it. Finally it slithered from the water and escaped into the weeds.

Some of my stubborn pride slowly melted away. I was sorry for turning on Brad the way I had. I knew I shouldn't have turned the whole Tiffany thing into such a big deal. It had been a long time since the two of us had had a heated confrontation. Mentally I reproved myself for flaring up. "He's leaving in a little over a month," I grumbled to myself, "and this is how I get ready to tell him good-bye." I stood up, knowing I should apologize as soon as he came up the hill.

A chilly wisp of wind brushed past me. I looked around. A few dark clouds hung on top of the mountain. I remembered Mom's comment about a cold front moving in. I glanced at my watch. It was 7:02, past time to turn the water down. Brad should have been in sight by now. I could hear the faint, low growl of the tractor engine, but it seemed distant and sluggish. Certain that Brad would appear at any moment, I pulled the headgate up, turning the water down. A gush of water started down the hill toward the garden. Grass and weeds grew in the ditch, so even though there was a good incline, the water's descent was sluggish. It would take several minutes for the water to even reach the garden.

Frustrated and impatient by Brad's slowness in bringing the tractor up the hill, I started back toward the garden, trotting easily. As I pushed down through the weeds and brush and approached that last bend between the two ridges, a stab of panic cut through me. The tractor was perched precariously off the trail, almost upside down, its two huge rear wheels grinding slowly. The engine choked and sputtered.

"Brad!" I yelled, feeling a staggering lurch deep in my gut. Breaking into a full sprint, I charged toward the overturned tractor. I tripped over a protruding root and took a diving spill, scuffing my face, arms, and hands, but as soon as I hit the ground, I was up again, running.

The soft dirt of the ditch bank had crumbled under the weight of the tractor, and the huge right rear wheel had slipped downward. The bulky, awkward weight of the tractor had caused it to slip over the edge, roll half a turn, and land on its side and top.

Leaping down the embankment, I landed shakily on the soft dirt that had crumbled into the ditch under the weight of the tractor. I scrambled around the rear wheels and found Brad lying face down in the dirt, the lower half of his body pinned beneath the overturned tractor.

"Brad!" I yelled, dropping to my knees in front of his head.

Brad pushed his head and shoulders up a few inches. His face was a pale, grayish hue, powdered with dirt. His lips were thin and drawn, but he managed a weak smile. "So much for me knowing how to drive," he grunted, trying to suck in air through his open mouth. "I shouldn't have been so stubborn."

Flooded with sudden relief that he was talking and conscious, I touched his arm. In turn he gripped my hand, leaned his forehead on the back of my hand, and shook his head. "I didn't even get close to the edge. Honest," he wheezed, half laughing, half moaning. He coughed and grimaced. "I was trying to be careful, and then the side of the trail gave way. Everything just crumbled, and it all seemed to happen in slow motion." He wet his lips and closed his eyes. "I stayed on as long as I could, trying to keep the tractor from rolling." He grinned weakly. "When I jumped, my bootlace hung up on the clutch pedal. I fell flat on my face."

"You can't even jump off a tractor," I muttered, attempting to joke but feeling no humor, only a gut-wrenching panic. Still gripping Brad's hand, I looked around. The tractor lay upside down at an angle in the ditch. Two or three tons of dirt had caved in and now filled the ditch bottom, with the tractor in front of it. The rear fender lay across Brad's hips and lower back. "How do you feel?" I questioned tensely.

Brad lay still for a moment as though considering the question. "I'm not sure." He grit his teeth. "I can feel my feet." He seemed to concentrate. "I'm moving my toes." He wet his lips again and panted a moment. "I don't think anything's broken, but I'm sure nailed down."

"The ground's soft here," I said optimistically. Both of us studied the ground, which was mostly the crumbled dirt from the bank. The bulky weight of the tractor had pressed Brad's lower body into this soft soil, probably saving him from being crushed. "You're going to be all right, Brad. Once we get this tractor off you, you'll be fine. A few bruises and scrapes maybe." I smiled. "You'll still make it to the dance tonight."

"I think I'll be a little stiff to dance. You'll have to take Tiffany for me."

I forced a laugh and shook my head. Suddenly I smelled the gasoline, and a red light of panic flared in my brain. Gasoline dripped from above onto Brad's neck and back. Some had even gotten onto my hands. A single spark could transform the tractor, Brad, and me into a billowing, explosive inferno. Brad must have sensed the danger at the same time I did. "Shut off the engine," he gasped.

Crawling and clawing my way around the tractor, I groped frantically for the key. My fingers brushed against it. Trembling, I grabbed and turned the key. The engine died. For a moment I remained transfixed, my fingers still gripping the key. I pressed my eyes closed and tried to think. I needed help. *Now!*

"Chris, are you still there?" Snapping from my shocked stupor, I crawled back to Brad. "What's that noise?" he asked.

I heard a hissing sizzle. Looking around, I saw to my horror that gasoline was dripping onto the hot exhaust pipe. Cold fear tore at my insides. If the gasoline ignited, Brad, soaked as he was, would roast alive inside a raging ball of fire. "You just hang in there," I said, looking away from the exhaust pipe, not wanting to panic him. "I'll get you out of here."

Brad's fingers dug and clawed at the soft dirt in front of him. "Get it off me," he gasped.

I gripped Brad's two hands, my face inches from his. "I'll go to Jed Morris's place. He's got that front-end loader. With that and a jack we can raise this enough to pull you out." I was panting, gasping for breath. I wet my lips and swallowed hard. My mouth was dry. My tongue was a thick, parched piece of wood in my mouth. "I'll be back before you know it."

Brad held onto my hands, his fingers pressing intently into the back of them. "I don't know if I'm going to make it, Chris."

I closed my eyes. "I should've driven this thing," I muttered, fighting off a sickening wave of guilty regret. "It was *my* job. Now you're paying for my mistake."

"It was going to cave in no matter who drove. Better me than you."

"I could have at least jumped off without getting my bootlaces wrapped around the clutch pedal," I said, trying to smile but failing. "Look, nothing's broken, so you're going to be okay. It'll hurt until we get this piece of junk off you, but everything's going to be all right."

Brad shook his head and tried to chuckle, but he was fighting off pain. "Maybe you could have jumped farther than me, but you would have probably landed on your head and broken your neck." His weak, hoarse laugh changed into a cough and then a gasp. "Something tells me I won't be running that marathon."

"You'll run it, and I'll be there beside you," I promised.

He coughed. "You'll have to run without me. You'll do it, won't you?"

I nodded my head and blinked back tears. "I'll run. I promise. But you'll run too," I countered fiercely. "You might run hunched over, looking like you're a hundred years old, but you'll run." I tried to tug my hands from his white-knuckled grip.

"Chris," he wheezed. It was hard for him to raise his head to look into my face, but he made the effort. "Chris," he repeated, wincing and closing his eyes. "I'm proud of you, Chris."

I didn't know how long it had been since I'd tumbled down the embankment. It seemed like forever, but it had probably been only three minutes. Stripping off my watch, I pushed it into Brad's hands. "Give me fifteen minutes and I'll be back with help. Then you'll be out of here."

"You always were an optimist, Chris."

"Fifteen minutes, Brad."

He smiled up at me through his pain, his face a grayish, pinched mask. "I'm not going anywhere." He swallowed and coughed. "But don't use that as an excuse to take your time."

CHAPTER TWELVE

Fifteen minutes wasn't enough to save Brad. I went for help, but even as I left him pinned beneath the tractor, I knew he wouldn't survive. And as neighbors and paramedics struggled to extricate Brad using shovels, jacks, and a front-end loader, I couldn't bear to watch.

Snatching one of the extra shovels, I abandoned the accident scene and escaped to the garden with a single dark purpose. Angry and distraught, I madly lashed out at the garden. Wielding the shovel in a morbid, irrational act of destruction, I ripped and tore indiscriminately at the ground, the head ditches, and some of the plants. I wished only to destroy the place in retaliation for Brad's death. Finally exhausted, shaking, and gasping for breath, I cast the shovel down, sank to my hands and knees and wept bitterly, pounding the ground with clenched fists and asking *why* between sobs.

I don't know how long I stayed in the garden, but as I gradually emerged from a numbing mist of emotions, I knew intuitively that they had taken Brad away. Sluggishly struggling from my grief-induced stupor, I felt desperate to find him. Wanting to avoid the spot of the accident, I took a circuitous route to the house.

Someone had driven the Chevy back to the barn. Taking it, I drove down the canyon toward McKay Hospital, illogically clinging to a thin, impossible shred of hope that Brad might have survived in spite of everything. I knew it would require a miracle, but a miracle seemed only fair. Brad was good enough for a miracle.

As I clung unreasonably to Brad's goodness, I was haunted by my own imperfections. In those final, crucial moments immediately prior to the accident, I had carelessly harbored jealous anger and lashed out at him. I certainly lacked the goodness to call down a miracle. Had my life been snuffed out—that would have been arguably fair. I shuddered guiltily while I struggled to find resolution, fairness, and logic to what had happened, but regardless of how I trifled with the scale of justice and fairness, nothing worked in Brad's favor.

I didn't ever find Brad or the family. I don't remember the places I visited, but partway through the seemingly endless night, a cold wind laced with an icy rain numbed me. I remember thinking that it would freeze that night, and I was glad because a freeze would certainly finish off the garden, and I loathed the garden.

I drove aimlessly, not returning to the house until three o'clock in the morning. Mom and Dad were still up, agonizing over Brad and worrying about me. They were searching for answers too, but disoriented in a kaleidoscope of guilty frustration, anger, and a sense of utter unfairness, I retreated from family contact. Sleep, brought on by sheer exhaustion, was my only escape.

For three days the skies over Eden were gray and overcast. Then Wednesday, the day of the funeral, the sun emerged, warming the valley. A few fleecy clouds brushed across the tree-covered hills while the rest of the sky was a clear, serene blue, accentuating the verdant lushness of the valley itself.

I sat on the lawn in the shade of a quaking aspen that grew in the southeast corner of the grounds surrounding the Eden/Liberty chapel, a small white-brick church, not so unlike hundreds of other Mormon meetinghouses. Green lawn, shrubs, trees, and a few freshly planted petunias adorned the premises. Immediately to the north of the church parking lot was a small acre field of alfalfa where the hissing blast of silver sprinklers sounded a refreshing chorus. When the breeze shifted just right, a thin, watery mist drifted in my direction.

South of the church and across the road was Snowcrest Junior High, where a soccer game was enthusiastically underway. How could people play soccer today when the white hearse in front of the church conjured a different mood? I found it hard to comprehend that today people could play, laugh, joke, and just plain live.

The air was filled with a rich cocktail of smells from the fields, the meadows, and a hundred yards and gardens—clover, flowers, lilacs, honeysuckle, and more. This was Brad's kind of day, a day that begged to be seized with reckless excitement and energy.

"Chris." I recognized Tiffany's voice and heard her soft footsteps brush across the grass till she was behind me. "I thought I'd find you out here."

"I remember Grandpa Huish's funeral," I remarked, as much to myself as to Tiffany. "Brad wanted me to sneak into the kitchen and rip off a chocolate cake with white coconut frosting, one the Relief Society had collected for the family dinner. He promised to stand guard." I smiled wryly. "You know how persuasive Brad could be."

"A whole cake?" Tiffany questioned. I knew she was smiling in spite of herself.

"Aunt Bethany caught me and threatened to make the whole thing a federal case. She chewed on me till I produced a couple of genuine tears to prove my remorse."

"And where was Brad?"

"He saw her coming and hid. By the time Aunt Bethany finished chewing on me, I was sniffling and blubbering for desecrating Grandpa's funeral. I was sure that when I died and went to heaven, Grandpa would never speak to me because I had tried to steal his funeral cake."

I sighed deeply. "After Aunt Bethany stomped away, Brad put his arm around me and whispered, 'At my funeral, everybody will have all the chocolate cake they want.'" I smiled fondly, remembering. "We should have a great big chocolate cake with white coconut frosting out here. And invite all the kids."

Tiffany laughed quietly. "There's been a steady stream of people," she pointed out gently. "Some of Snow's football team showed up." She touched my shoulder. I turned and looked up at her as she stood behind me. She was wearing a navy blue dress that hit her midcalf. She wore a gold necklace and tiny gold earrings. Her blue eyes were red and puffy, and she clutched a white handkerchief. "May I sit down?" She pointed to a spot of shade next to me. I nodded, and she put her hand on my shoulder and slowly sank beside me, tucking her skirt around her legs.

I had hardly spoken to Tiffany since that day in the garden. She had made several attempts to talk, but I had shut her out as I had everyone else. "I'll miss him, Chris," she spoke, ducking her head and pressing the handkerchief to her mouth. "I still can't believe he's gone." She caught her breath and leaned against me, slipping her arm through mine. She laughed weakly, sadly. "He used to tell me that freckles turned into warts once you hit puberty. I knew he was lying, but he said it so convincingly that he made me wonder. I'd study myself in the mirror, horrified that he might be right. When I spotted my first zit, I almost had a nervous breakdown, thinking it was Brad's promised plague of warts.

"Of course, he wasn't always a tease," she continued, musing. "While I was growing up, I had pretty much accepted that beauty wasn't one of God's gifts to me. I was barely thirteen and had dressed up to go out to dinner with Susan Blakeslee's family for her birthday. Mom had fixed my hair. I was waiting for Susan to pick me up when Brad showed up at the house to return a lesson manual to Mom." She paused and stared down at the grass. "I waited for him to make a crack about what I was wearing or how Mom had fixed my hair. I knew that when he did, it was going to crush me. Instead he said, 'You know, Tiff, you're actually kind of pretty sometimes.'" Tiffany laughed. "Maybe that's not much of a compliment as far as great compliments go, but it meant a whole lot to me that day coming from Brad."

She seemed to know I had nothing to say, so, brushing her hand across the grass in front of us, she went on. "Everybody at Weber High thought Brad was *the* man. His sophomore year, when he first became Weber's starting quarterback, all the girls, even the juniors and seniors, thought he was so *very* fine. Here I was a lowly freshman, and I didn't just know Brad Huish, I hung around with him. He came over to my place to watch TV, to play ball. We worked out together. We walked to church together. I mean, we were *best* friends. And, of course, I was in love with him and planned to marry him. In my dreams."

I looked out at the green, pine-covered mountains. "Remember when Brad and I were going to take you hitchhiking?"

Tiffany laughed. "We were going to start here in Eden with a bed-roll, a few changes of clothes, and five hundred dollars each. And we were going to see if we could make it to the East Coast and back." She swallowed. "When I mentioned it to Mom, she practically had a stroke, telling me how I'd get beaten up, robbed, murdered, and worse." She laughed. "I was still pretty naive, but I was shocked that she was even worried because the whole plan seemed perfectly logical to me. After all, I would have had Brad and you to protect me."

Tiffany pressed her handkerchief to her face and rested her free hand on the back of mine. Slowly I turned my hand over and took hers. "Shall we go in?" she encouraged, holding my hand even tighter. "They'll close the casket soon. You'll want to say good-bye."

I took a deep breath to steady my voice. I had been the last person to be with Brad, but most of those final moments were blank, locked behind ironlike, impenetrable mental doors, doors that I had slammed closed. I could pry open those dark mental doors, but I had no desire to conjure up Brad's tragic end. He was gone. That was tragedy enough. "I don't need to see him in a casket," I said morosely.

"Chris, I wish I could . . ." She hesitated and smoothed her dress. "I've tried to come up with all the right answers—"

"Since Saturday I've been trying to sort through this whole puzzle," I interrupted, shaking my head and snatching at a tuft of grass. I rolled the blades of grass between my fingers and let them flutter to the ground.

"Sometimes we just can't understand at first, Chris."

I smiled bitterly. "Do you know what Brad was going to do a month from today?" I questioned, squinting out to where the sun baked the asphalt parking lot. "He planned to walk through the doors at the MTC."

"The Lord has something else for him."

"The Lord was the one who called him to Mexico. That's what He wanted him to do."

"The Lord needs him someplace else."

"So why didn't He take him before he got his call, before we all had our hopes up?" I shook my head. "How much sense does that make?"

Tiffany touched my arm again. I grabbed another tuft of grass between my thumb and forefinger and, one by one, dropped the blades to the ground. My jaw clamped tight while I stared ahead. I felt a sudden, painful emotion explode inside me that started in my chest and expanded through my whole system. Closing my eyes and taking a couple of deep breaths, I whispered, "I loved him, but I had a hard time telling him. Especially that last day."

"He knew it, Chris." Tiffany glanced at her watch and then toward the church. "We'll miss the family prayer if we don't go soon. Come on." She gave me a gentle nudge as she pushed up from the grass and brushed at her dress. "Your mom asked me to sit with the family."

I smiled plaintively. "She said she was going to."

"Don't make me sit alone, Chris." She touched the back of my head and walked away.

I missed the family prayer, but as the family filed from the Relief Society room behind Brad's casket, I stepped next to Tiffany. She reached out and took my hand as we walked to the chapel. Even after we sat down, she continued to hold it.

At first I tried to concentrate on the service, but I found my mind wandering, remembering the Brad Huish that only I knew. The music, the prepared remarks, the tributes, and the warm recollections seemed disjointed and confusing because I found myself unable to concentrate on them. Bishop McFadden concluded the service by speaking of Brad's aborted earthly mission and of his new mission call in another place. I wanted to take comfort in that, but that comfort was elusive. Brad was still dead, his dreams unfulfilled, and I was still alone—not for just two years, but for the rest of my life. The choir sang "O My Father," and my Uncle Roy offered the benediction.

By the end of the service, I was numb, fighting to keep my thoughts from the accident and trying to bring resolution to my own life. Suddenly I wanted to escape, to be away from the congregation. I didn't want to talk. I didn't want reassurance. I just wanted to hurt alone. What I felt so poignantly no one else could possibly understand. And the last thing I wanted was to try to explain that to someone else.

I left the chapel and started toward the truck. I had cleaned it the day before, cleaned it better than it had ever been cleaned, for Brad—not that it would make much difference to him now, but it was a small gesture I wanted to make.

"Can I ride with you to the cemetery?" Tiffany called to me as I reached the truck.

I opened the door and ran my finger down the side of the steering wheel. "I'm not going," I spoke quietly.

"You're a pallbearer."

Tiffany touched my shoulder. Slowly her fingers slid down my arm until they reached my hand. She took my hand in both of hers.

At that moment I wanted to hold Tiffany and tell her how much she meant to me, how much I needed her, but there was no way I could explain to her that my last moments with Brad had turned bleakly bitter because I had selfishly wanted her. "I need time to sort through a few things," I responded huskily, swallowing. "A few days ago my whole life was neatly organized. Now everything's busted and scattered."

"Chris, you can't change what happened to Brad, but you can go on living. That's what Brad would want. He's fine where he is. You have to believe what Bishop McFadden said about the Lord's plan of happiness," she pled with me.

"I didn't hear much of anything," I muttered bitterly.

"But don't you believe?"

"I suppose I've always believed, but I believed hypothetically. This is real, and it's harder to believe when it's real. What now?"

"Your mission. That's a start."

"I don't know if I can. Not right away. That's part of the puzzle that's broken all over the place." I shook my head. "So much of what I've dreamed of doing was tied up with Brad. I don't want to go back to places and things Brad and I had planned." I faced Tiffany. Her eyes were red. "Go with the others," I suggested gently.

Tiffany swallowed and touched a tear with the tip of her finger. She started to leave and then stopped. "I'll go home with you," she offered. "I want to be with you, Chris."

I wanted her to stay with me, but my guilt prevented my saying so. I shook my head. "Go with the others."

She turned and left. Arriving home, I changed to my work clothes and went to the barn to straighten things there. The tiny Eden cemetery, located on a small rise in the middle of fields and pastures, was only three-quarters of a mile beyond our barn. I could have climbed to the loft and watched the graveside service from there. I was tempted, but instead I immersed myself in work.

CHAPTER THIRTEEN

The day after Brad's funeral, I started work with Wilson Tanner, a friend of Dad's and a subcontractor who hung drywall. I had never figured that hanging a few sheets of drywall would be a challenge. Until I did it. Wilson worked long hours and maintained a killer pace. We didn't knock off work that first day until almost six, and by then I was exhausted. My arms, shoulders, and back throbbed. I was dusty and sweaty. The only thing I wanted to do was to shower and crash into bed. Each succeeding day was the same.

Those long, hard hours became my routine. Wilson even worked me Saturdays. I went to church on Sundays, but timed my entry so that I could sit on the back row where I didn't have to speak to anyone. As soon as the meetings were over, I slipped out and headed home. The remaining part of the day I drove around the valley or hiked up the mountain so that I could be alone and undisturbed.

Mom, Dad, Randy, and Lisa tried to draw me out of my self-imposed cloister, but I ignored them. Several times Tiffany stopped by, but usually I wasn't home or I conveniently disappeared.

One Tuesday evening, a couple of weeks into my job, I was driving back to Eden and I was exhausted. Turning off Harrison Boulevard and starting toward the canyon, I passed two joggers. All of a sudden tears came to my eyes. I had never felt Brad's compulsion to run a marathon, but after passing those two joggers, it was as though something in my brain pounded a message through my nerves—*Run the marathon. For Brad!* I had promised him that I would.

The rest of the way home I contemplated Brad's marathon, finally resolving to run it just as he had planned, the last Saturday of June—not for recognition or glory, only to prove I could.

As soon as I reached home, I changed into a pair of jogging shorts, a T-shirt, and running shoes and headed down the road toward North Fork. Even though I was tired from work, it felt good to run. The warm breeze against my face and my deep, steady breathing were exhilarating in a strange way. It had been two weeks since I had jogged, but I discovered that I hadn't lost my rhythm or stamina. I ran close to four miles, but I felt I could have gone forever.

When I returned to the house, I was still energized. Dressed in my running clothes, I decided to change the oil in the Chevy while making plans for the big run two weeks away.

"Hello, Chris."

I pulled out from under the hood and turned. Tiffany stood there with her hands in the back pockets of her faded denim jeans. She wore a loose-fitting knit shirt and a pair of flat leather sandals.

"Hello, Tiffany," I greeted guardedly, reaching for a rag and wiping the grease and dirt from my hands.

"I haven't seen you around much," she observed, stepping over to the truck and looking down at the engine. She smiled wanly. "Unless I count the times you slip out of church as soon as the last amen is said. I've even stopped by here." She shrugged. "Maybe you didn't know."

I looked away.

She reached up and touched the open hood. "You must make pretty good company for yourself. I always thought you were pretty boring." She laughed and tossed a rag at me. "Just kidding," she quickly added. "I passed you coming up the canyon a couple of days ago. You didn't even wave. But of course you always were stuck up."

I wiped my hands on the rag she had thrown me. "I didn't see you."

She turned her back to the engine, leaned against the grill, and folded her arms. "I know you've wanted time to think. I figured that eventually you'd drop by and see me when you were ready." She breathed deeply and smiled plaintively. "I guess I got tired of waiting for you."

"I'm sorry," I muttered, embarrassed and a bit ashamed.

She shook her head. "Don't shut everyone out, Chris." I wadded up the greasy cloth and tossed it on top of the toolbox at my feet. "We've always talked, shared, helped each other out."

"It's different now."

"You mean *you're* different now."

I shrugged. "I suppose that it ends up being the same thing."

"No, it's not the same thing," Tiffany spoke with a gentle edge to her voice. "I know you miss Brad. We all do. Maybe not in the same way you do, but you're not the first person to lose someone you cared about. You can't just stop living. If you spend too much time alone, you'll forget how important it is to have people around you who care. You'll get so tied up in hurting that you won't remember what it's like to live. Have you looked around lately?" With a sweep of her hand and arm she motioned to everything around us. "Things are beautiful this time of year. Would Brad want you to close your eyes to all this? Do you think he's stopped living?"

I thought a moment, leaning against the fender. "People talk like Brad's accident was supposed to happen, like it was part of the great plan. Maybe Brad wasn't supposed to die. It didn't have to happen, Tiffany. That dirt along the ditch could have held one more time. How much of a miracle would it take to keep his bootlace from getting tangled on the clutch pedal?"

Tiffany shook her head. "Do you think you're the only one who wants to make a few minor adjustments?" She shrugged and looked at me. "This is real life we're talking about," she said, exasperated. "Not something we just dream about. We can't always have things the way we want."

"I know that," I grumbled.

"No, Chris, I don't think you do. Maybe hypothetically you know." Her words were a harsh indictment, but her tone was gentle. "The Lord has a plan, and the more people try to remake it to fit their special situations, the more it falls apart. We can't expect little miracles all along the way to avoid the rough places. You don't remember doing it, but you agreed to this plan, just like Brad, me, and everybody else. You can't get in the middle of a race and suddenly say you don't want to run. You *are* always running."

Her words stung me. I turned back to the truck and started pouring oil into the engine. After putting in three quarts of oil, I grabbed the oily rag and wiped my hands. "Brad had so much to do," I said softly. "Good things. He was giving two years of his life for the Lord. But do you have any idea how much he wanted to play ball at Snow this fall?

That's why he kept going back and forth. He was driving me up the wall because he wouldn't make up his mind." My voice started to rise. "He knew he should go on that mission, but he wanted to see what it was like to play college ball. Things were going perfectly for him, and he could have made it as a college quarterback—his dream. That's when he decided that he was going to put the Lord first. He was going to serve that mission—and he was going to give that mission his very best. He was ready to go out and . . ." I stopped and lowered my head and closed my eyes. "What purpose was there to him . . ." I wet my lips and swallowed, " . . . dying down there in the garden? If he had decided to play ball this fall, none of this would have happened."

I reached for another quart of oil and unscrewed the cap. Tiffany held her hand out and took the cap from me. For several minutes we worked in silence, finishing up the oil change. Tiffany was the one to finally speak. "How do you like working for Wilson Tanner?" she questioned, trying to divert my thoughts from Brad.

"I'm not as stiff as I was at the end of that first day. Wilson keeps me hopping, though. I don't have time to . . ." I heaved a sigh, ". . . to feel sorry for myself."

Tiffany took the rag from the fender. "I want to help you. If you think of anything . . ." She wiped her hands on the rag and started to go.

"I'm going to run Brad's marathon."

Tiffany stopped and stared. "Run his marathon?" she asked incredulously.

"It's something he wanted me to do." I closed the truck's hood and leaned my forearms on top of it. "Brad always figured I needed to do something athletic." I smiled and shook my head. "He was afraid my brain would explode if I didn't do something to take my mind off studying." I looked toward the corral and became serious, almost sad, as I remembered. "I don't know why, but Brad was determined that I run this marathon. I'm going to do it for him."

"Do you have any idea how long a marathon is?"

"A little over twenty-six miles."

She smiled without disguising her doubt. "You don't just go out and run a marathon, Chris." She raked her fingers through her hair. "The first one to run it was some Greek guy three thousand years ago.

He was taking a message from a battlefield to a place called Marathon, a little over twenty-six miles away. He ran the distance—and dropped dead as soon as he got there."

"And you think I'll drop dead?" I kidded.

"How many times have you run twenty-six miles straight?"

"Nobody runs twenty-six miles for practice. Today I ran a good four miles. Even I was surprised by how good I felt. Two weeks from Saturday is when he planned to run, so I've still got a little time to do some serious training. I can do it, Tiffany. I can feel it in here," I said, pressing my fist to my chest. "It won't be easy, but I'll do it."

"And then what?"

I looked at her, surprised. "What do you mean?"

"What happens after you run? Will that put Brad behind you? Will you stop hurting?"

I considered her question but didn't answer. I wanted to say that as soon as I crossed the finish line I'd be over the hurt, the disappointment, the depression. All I managed to say was, "It'll make a difference. I'll make it make a difference."

"The Saturday that Brad worked in the garden, he asked me to help him with the marathon," Tiffany remarked, not looking at me. "He wanted me to ride ahead and give him water at intervals. Can I help you, or do you have to do this whole thing by yourself?"

"Can you be ready at quarter to five two weeks from Saturday?"

"Do I have to be wide awake?" she smiled.

For a moment we studied each other. I had missed her the last two weeks, and it felt good to have her near. "I don't care if you're awake or asleep as long as you can hand me a cup of water every three or four miles."

She nodded and started walking away. Then she stopped and faced me. "Chris, I hope this marathon does what you want it to."

"Do you miss him?" I wanted my words to be a simple question; they came more as an accusation.

She thought a moment and then smiled weakly. "Chris, I miss both of you." Slowly she walked away.

* * *

Pale yellow rays of light streaked the eastern sky as I climbed into the truck that last Saturday in June. The sun hadn't peeked over the mountain, so a chill lingered in the air. I felt tense, rankled by a rumbling of anticipation in the pit of my stomach. When I first considered the marathon, it was just an idea. This morning it was an impending agony, something I couldn't escape unless I surrendered my commitment.

Tiffany was sitting on her front step with a jacket draped about her shoulders when I drove up. She climbed in beside me. "It's not supposed to be chilly in June," she remarked with a bit of a smile while her teeth chattered slightly. "Don't you want to wait till it warms up?"

"I'm not worried about freezing. An hour from now I'll be sweating like a horse."

"Are you ready?"

I smiled. "You're never really ready for a marathon. It's an insanity run—you have to be crazy to run it in the first place. How do you get ready for something like that?"

I handed her the hand-drawn map Brad had taped to the mirror. Just south of the church and Snowcrest Junior High was the Maverik store. There the main road forked, one road going west of Pineview Reservoir, the other going east. Brad had planned to start at the Maverik store, take the west road, cross the dam, make the wide loop around Huntsville, and then head back toward Eden, coming from the east fork. He'd then planned to head to Liberty, which was a mile north of the Maverik. From there he was going to head up to North Fork Park to finish the marathon. He had marked his course with half a dozen X's.

"Can you make sense of it?" I asked Tiffany.

"Brad explained the whole thing to me. The X's are where you get your drinks. And you don't want to stop," she added, anticipating my instructions. "I'm supposed to jog along beside you with a couple of cups and hand them to you. Sounds easy enough."

"For you," I said, grinning.

We stopped the truck in front of the Maverik store and climbed out. I spent five minutes stretching my legs and loosening my muscles. I took a couple swallows of water and then rinsed my mouth out and spat into the weeds alongside the road. Taking several deep gulps of air, I jogged in place for a moment, trying to calm the flutter in my stomach.

"There should be a crowd here to cheer you on," Tiffany stated, looking around as though anticipating a few spectators. "It doesn't seem right that you run something like this without crowds of people along the route clapping and shouting words of encouragement."

"Brad wasn't doing it for the glory—just to prove something to himself. And to me."

"Shall I time you?"

I thought a moment and then nodded, adding with a wry grin, "But the only thing that matters is whether I finish." I moved to the starting spot. "You tell me when," I muttered.

Tiffany stepped in front of me. "You forgot something." She took my face in her hands, pulled me toward her, and kissed me on the lips. "Now you're ready," she whispered, smiling.

"You'll make me lose my concentration."

She blushed and looked down at the watch she had taken off her wrist and now held in her hand. "You don't think I came out here just to watch you race, did you?" She grinned and raised her hand, then dropped it rapidly, calling out at the same time, "Go!"

The first half mile was down a gradual incline, but then the road climbed the low foothills immediately west of the reservoir. I did my best to calm the nervous jitters in my stomach, to regulate my breathing, and to establish a steady stride. At first I panicked because it seemed as though I was suddenly tired. I forced myself to take deep, even breaths, and gradually my nerves settled down. My breathing became regular, and I felt a surge of energy and a keen sense of victory as my strides steadied into an easy, loping rhythm.

The first four miles were along the west side of the reservoir. It was a refreshing jog with the green hills to my right and the deep blue waters of the reservoir to my left. A few early boaters were launching their fancy crafts, but for the most part the water's surface remained a serene, glassy blue mirror catching the reflection of the azure sky. My breathing was deep and even, and by now the jitters were completely gone, replaced by a reassuring determination. The morning was cool, but sweat beaded on my forehead and trickled down the sides of my face.

The first water station was at four miles, just north of the dam. When I was still a quarter mile away I spotted the truck with Tiffany leaning against it. As I approached she held the cups of cold water out as she began to jog next to me. I snatched one and drank as I ran. Half the water spilled down my chin and onto my shirt, but the cool moisture felt good.

"Are you feeling all right?" Tiffany asked, taking my empty cup and handing me another one. I nodded and wiped my mouth with the back of my hand. "Are your muscles loose?"

"I'm fine."

"No cramps?"

I shook my head.

"I'll meet you at the Mountain Green turnoff. That's the eight-mile mark," she called after me as she slowed to a stop and I continued on. A moment later she drove past me in the truck. I crossed the dam and for a moment wished she were still jogging next to me.

Jogging along the highway toward Huntsville, I gazed down upon the cool freshness of the water below and thought of Brad. There was a sudden ache as I remembered his enthusiasm. "Why a marathon?" I had questioned.

His contagious grin had spread across his tanned face. "When you choose something, you want to choose the biggest and the best. What's longer than a marathon?"

Knowing he'd planned to run without spectators, I had jokingly questioned, "And what if you break the record? Don't you want your name in the record book?"

He had become serious. "We're not doing this so we'll end up on the cover of *Sports Illustrated*. We're doing it to prove something to ourselves. You've got to have a fire in your gut for this race, Chris, or you'll quit."

Now, as I spotted Tiffany at the Mountain Green turnoff, my breath was more labored and there was a tired stiffness in my legs, especially in my left Achilles tendon. I had strained it several weeks ago on one of my early morning jogs. Now it nagged at me again.

"You've run just over an hour and ten minutes," Tiffany called as I approached. She held up two cups of water. I grabbed the first, took a couple of gulps, and poured the rest on top of my head. Tiffany passed me the second cup. I took a swallow, swished the cool liquid in my mouth, and spat. Then, trying not to slosh the rest of the water, I drank between gulps of air.

"How do you feel?" Tiffany questioned.

"All right," I gasped. I didn't want to say anything about the stiffness in my legs or the shadow of exhaustion that I'd detected. It was too early in the race to be tired. The fatigue would pass. It had to.

"The next station is at the junction east of Huntsville. You'll take the road toward the monastery," she called as she fell behind. "That's only two more miles. I'll be waiting."

The sun was up now, driving away the last traces of morning coolness. I was sweating heavily, some of the brine trickling down into the corners of my eyes and causing an annoying burn. I wiped at my forehead and sides of my face with the back of my hands, since my sleeves and the front of my T-shirt were soaked.

My upper legs were chafing from where they were rubbing together. My breathing was still deep and steady but was becoming more labored with each inhale. My legs ate away at the pavement, but more effort was required now.

Tiffany waited for me at the junction. I gulped my water and then pounded my way down the road to the monastery. Up to this point I had always been able to catch refreshing glimpses of the reservoir. Now I was running away from it, going past less refreshing houses and fields.

Two miles down this road, I turned left, ran a quarter mile or so, and then turned left again, taking a second road back to the main highway, the highway returning to Eden. By the time I returned to the main highway, I had run sixteen miles, and the reservoir was once more in sight.

Earlier the blue waters of Pineview Reservoir had proved refreshing; now they taunted and tantalized me. I needed a drink, and Tiffany was still a quarter mile ahead. I longed for a tall, cold drink, not just a single cup. I imagined leaping into the cold, blue waters of the reservoir and gulping to my full satisfaction.

Tiffany met me with two cups fifty yards before I reached the truck. I gulped them down, splashing more water on my face. As we passed the truck, Tiffany snatched two more cups off the truck's hood and handed them to me. I tried to drink them, but I couldn't run and drink without sloshing half the water down my front or onto the ground.

"You're more than halfway," Tiffany encouraged. "Halfway was a couple miles back. You can do it, Chris. Just keep pushing yourself."

I sensed a touch of worry in her voice as she called out those last words. I wondered if I looked as bad as I felt. Up till then, my thoughts had drifted to Brad. Now, as the challenge of the marathon pressed in upon me with its intimidating force, my mind concentrated on the effort at hand, putting one foot in front of the other, sucking in huge gulps of air, and trying not to think about the sticky, burning thirst that was now a constant irritant.

The road now ran parallel to the reservoir. In places where there were inlets, the road actually passed over the water. I passed pastures where sprinklers shot crystal mists that intensified my thirst and made me even more conscious of the growing heat.

When I spotted the truck again, I was hurting. The slight irritation where my legs rubbed against each other had developed into a scorching burn. The muscles in both my legs were tired and stiff, and my left Achilles tendon was a constant throb. My eyes smarted as the sweat poured down the sides of my face. I longed for a towel—anything to wipe away the briny flood.

I came to the next water station sooner than I had anticipated. "I stopped at eighteen miles instead of nineteen," Tiffany explained. "You looked like you could use it. I'll set up every mile or so now."

I nodded my agreement as I drank and tried to cool myself.

"Are you going to be all right?"

I nodded again. "Don't do anything that will hurt you," she cautioned. "It's just a race."

"I'm going to finish it, Tiffany. Even if it kills me."

"If it kills you, it won't prove anything," she called after me, standing in the road. "Brad didn't plan to kill himself in this marathon."

I ignored her remark, pushing on with more determination than ever, trying to stoke the fire in my gut that Brad had described. I'd prove to Tiffany that I wouldn't stop till I crossed the mark scratched across the pavement eight miles ahead. Eight miles! The thought staggered me!

Relentlessly I pushed forward, my aches meshing torturously into one throbbing pain. A burning blister developed on the inside of my right foot. The Achilles tendon was now forcing me to limp. The chafing between my legs intensified with each step. It was impossible to get enough air into my lungs. And there was a dead heaviness in my legs that made them feel like wooden posts. My pace had slowed considerably.

Eden was just ahead, and I could see the top of our barn. I dreaded passing our house because I didn't want anyone there to see me. I also wondered if the sight of the house would tempt me to stop and give up the race altogether.

As I limped through the pain, I realized I had deceived myself into thinking that I was in shape. I obviously wasn't prepared for this. My body weakened, as did my determination. Each step seemed to extinguish the fires of resolve inside me.

"You're limping, Chris," were Tiffany's first words as she handed me the cup of water a quarter of a mile from my house.

"I'm fine," I growled. "How much farther?"

"This is nineteen miles. It's been almost three hours." Tiffany handed me another cup. "Nineteen miles is nothing to be ashamed of. There aren't many people who can last nineteen miles."

"A marathon is twenty-six miles, not nineteen," I snapped with as much angry energy as I could muster. "It doesn't mean anything if I stop now."

It was pure angry determination that pushed me down the road to the next water station. I passed my house and the town park, glaring straight ahead, seeing nothing but the black pavement in front of me. I was barely dragging along, not much faster than a hard walk, but I continued to jog, determined to prove that I would finish Brad's marathon.

When I reached the Maverik store, I clumsily dropped the first two cups of water. Tiffany raced ahead and grabbed two more. She dashed both of them into my face and down my front and then ran back and grabbed two more just as I was passing the truck. She held the first cup until she was sure I had it. I was breathing so deeply that I could hardly drink. Tiffany didn't protest or try to dissuade me. I wanted to stop for just a moment and drink without slopping half the water down my front, but I knew if I stopped, even for a few seconds, I'd never start again.

Between the twentieth and twenty-first mile my body completely gave out. In the distance I could see the wooden sign welcoming people to Liberty. As soon as I saw the sign, I told myself that I would at least reach Liberty. That wasn't the full twenty-six miles, but reaching Liberty would be a small triumph of sorts. But in the end, it was no use. It was as though I had used the very last drop of energy, and regardless of how much I wanted to go on, I couldn't. I had heard of people "hitting the wall," but I hadn't realized that it was so final, so definite. I staggered to the side of the road and sat down under a small tree.

As soon as I sat down, I knew I had to get up and move or my whole body would contort into a torturous cramp. I pushed myself to my feet and staggered about, trying to keep my legs moving. As I walked, I wondered if I could force myself to walk the last five or six miles, but the mere thought of continuing another six miles, running or walking, was more than I could bear. No amount of personal con-demnation could force me to push on.

"Are you all right?" Tiffany called to me, jumping from the truck and putting her arm around me to steady me.

I didn't want Tiffany to see me like this and to look at me with pity. I didn't want her to praise me for making it almost twenty-one miles, because nothing short of the twenty-six meant anything. And I had no desire to try again. Ever.

"I couldn't do it," I muttered. "It didn't matter how much I wanted it—it didn't matter how much fire I had in my guts. I couldn't do it."

"Get in the truck."

I shook my head. "I need to walk or my muscles will cramp."

Grimacing, I limped alongside the road for ten minutes. Finally Tiffany helped me into the truck. "I'll get you home."

"I want to drive the rest of the course," I mumbled. "I don't want to go home yet, not like this. When I get home, I want to walk into the house without someone carrying me."

"But—" she started to protest.

"Just do it my way this once," I cut her off.

Tiffany hesitated and then muttered, "I thought we'd done it your way all along."

We drove the remaining six miles of the course without speaking. Afterwards we drove around the reservoir and through Huntsville. I let the air from the open window wash over me.

"I thought I could do it," I remarked after a long silence. "I really did. Even when I started hurting, I just knew I was going to finish. I couldn't imagine it any other way."

"You did fine. You don't have to beat yourself up."

"But Brad—"

"You're not Brad," she cut me off softly but firmly, heaving a sigh. "You've never been Brad." Then she added in a more sympathetic tone, "Brad didn't run the marathon either. He just tried to do his best. That's what you did too."

"He would have finished it."

"You don't know that." She shook her head. "You were sure you'd finish it. But it doesn't matter one way or the other. It was just a race."

Tiffany parked the truck by the barn. She offered to help me into the house, but I declined. She nodded her head slowly, turned, and started walking for home while I staggered into the house, opening and closing the front door quietly, hoping everyone in the family was busy and wouldn't see me. I made it up the stairs and into the shower without being noticed.

When I finally crashed into bed twenty minutes later, I was exhausted. More than anything, I wanted to sleep. I'd never get enough sleep, no matter how long I lay in bed. My eyes closed, and the world around me disappeared.

CHAPTER FOURTEEN

It was almost five o'clock in the evening when I shook loose from the all-consuming sleep gripping me. I moaned and stretched against the stiffness in my legs and feet. Gingerly I rolled off the bottom bunk and pushed myself to a standing position before taking a couple of unsteady steps. The raw, chafed area of my thighs made me wince and walk bowlegged.

Slipping on a pair of sweat pants and a T-shirt, I crept down the stairs in my bare feet and shuffled into the kitchen. Standing next to the sink, I poured myself a glass of orange juice and sipped it slowly. I hadn't eaten all day, but the emptiness in my stomach was overwhelmed by a consuming dry thirst, and the orange juice didn't quench it very well. I gulped three glasses of water and then filled up the glass with orange juice again before walking out into the shade of the backyard. Still holding my drink, I dropped into one of the lounge chairs, closed my eyes, and listened to the birds in the trees overhead.

The windows were open, and I heard Lisa call my name, then pound up the stairs, rap on my bedroom door, and call my name again. I didn't want to disrupt the tranquility of the moment and it was too much effort to call out to her, so I kept lying there silently with my eyes closed.

"Can't you answer?" Lisa exclaimed from my upstairs window overlooking the backyard. "I've been calling you. Someone's here to see you."

I opened my eyes. Lisa's face was pressed against the window screen. "Do I want to see this someone?" I asked tiredly.

"After I babied you and practically ran the race for you this morning, you'd better want to see me." The back screen door opened and closed, and Tiffany stepped out. "Do you need a doctor or a mortician?" she asked as she approached.

"Whichever one can make the pain stop."

She stood in front of me and studied me with amusement. "After watching you this morning, I was inspired to make a new commitment. I'm going to get in shape and run a marathon, so I need a jogging partner. I figured you'd be interested." She grinned mischievously.

"You're a real pal for asking."

"Don't you have this mad passion for running?"

"It took me thirty minutes to walk from my room to here. I hobble like an old man with hot sand in his pants. It's not a pretty sight."

She laughed. "Hey, let's see a demonstration. Jog across the lawn for me."

I took a sip of juice and set the glass down on the grass. "If you came to gloat over my misery," I said, smiling, "take a hike. If you want to show lots of sympathy, pull up a chair."

Tiffany pulled a lawn chair in front of me and sat down. "Are you sure you aren't faking all this?" She studied me and nodded. "You definitely look improved from this morning. That pale green tint you had didn't flatter your looks at all." She smiled slyly. "You don't seem quite so proud. Or ornery. That's a good change. Pain can do that to you."

I smiled weakly. "I love your brand of sympathy. You probably get a buzz going around knocking crippled old men out of their wheelchairs, too." I closed my eyes and shifted positions in the chair, moaning at the same time. "Anything that doesn't ache is numb."

"You're definitely more humble now. Maybe I can talk some sense into your head."

I rolled my eyes. "Please don't preach. I hurt too much for you to preach to me."

"That's the best time to preach to you because you have to listen. You've been moping around and sulking for the past few weeks, refusing to let anyone say 'boo' to you. Now that you're an invalid, you have to listen. Before coming over here, I decided that I was going to talk to you straight. You can get mad if you want," she said with casual indifference. "But in your crippled condition, you'll just have to sit there and take it."

"All right," I rasped. "What are you dying to tell me?"

She shrugged and smiled. "Give me a few minutes. I'll think of something." She leaned back in her chair. "Roberta and I are going to a movie in Salt Lake. Do you want to come?"

"Are you asking me on a date?" I teased.

"No. Actually, it's a charity project that Roberta and I want to do. You know, helping the downtrodden and the unfortunate."

I took another drink. "I don't feel like moving more than two inches from this chair." I peered momentarily at Tiffany and then closed my eyes. "I definitely don't have any ambition to do another marathon," I whispered. "But I do wish I could have finished the one this morning."

"It just wasn't your race," Tiffany sighed heavily.

I opened my eyes. "Tiffany," I responded impatiently, "I made it my race."

"Maybe you shouldn't have," she answered tiredly, leaning her head back. "Look," she said, suddenly sitting up and leaning forward, "Brad had his own races to run and his own trials to face. So do you. Maybe his race was being able to give up football and serve a mission." She hesitated and then added quietly, "And then face death. Perhaps yours is living after he's gone—without giving up and feeling sorry for yourself. We don't always get to choose our races. Sometimes they're just given to us."

I looked away, not wanting my melancholy mood to return.

"Everybody loved Brad," Tiffany observed gently. "Nobody wanted to see him go, but he was at peace, I think." She shifted her weight and tucked one of her legs under her while she smiled and slowly shook her head. Taking a deep breath, she gazed across the lawn away from me. "That last Saturday in the garden, Brad said, 'Tiff, I'm not perfect. Probably not in anything. That used to bother me some, but in the last few days I've come to realize that that's all right. The Lord will pick up the slack. I used to think that I had to do it by myself. I don't. Nobody does.'" Tiffany looked at me. "That's what gave him peace at the end." She sighed. "That Saturday, working in the garden meant a lot to Brad. Before you got there, he kept saying over and over, 'Tiffany, this whole place is a miracle, your and Chris's miracle.'"

"It was supposed to be *his* miracle," I muttered. "For his mission."

"And your mission," she came back ruefully. "Don't forget *your* mission. Forget the marathon. Do something about your mission. Save the garden. That's why you planted it."

"We planted the garden to help Brad, not kill him."

"Chris, the garden didn't kill anybody. It's still a good place."

"It won't grow anything now," I sighed. "I saw to that. And the frost finished what I didn't." I laughed humorlessly. "We were so worried about an early frost killing the garden, and then, when we weren't paying attention, something else killed Brad." There was a sudden tightness in my throat as that final scene in the garden—an experience I had confided to no one—forced its way into my mind. I fought to block it out. "This morning when I wanted to run those last six miles, I realized that no matter how hard I tried, I couldn't do it. It seemed unfair. Like Brad's death . . ." I murmured bitterly, clenching my teeth and closing my eyes. "That day I thought of all the miracles that were wasted."

"Wasted miracles?"

"When Mom was carrying Brad, she almost lost him. The doctors didn't think there was any way he was going to make it. Dad gave her a blessing, and she had a normal delivery. Then, when Brad was two, Dad backed out of the barn in a truck loaded with grain and ran right over him. He survived. The doctor just shook his head and said it was a miracle. When he was nine, we rode our bikes over to the reservoir. The water was high that year, and we found what we thought was a good swimming spot, even though neither one of us knew how to swim. We were splashing around in water up to our armpits, and then Brad charged farther out in the water. The next thing I knew, he just disappeared below the surface. There was a drop-off there that we didn't know about. A second later Brad bobbed to the surface, flailing his arms, choking and gasping for air, but he couldn't touch the bottom, and he was drifting farther out, away from me. I couldn't reach him without slipping off that same drop-off, so I just stood there, watching him drown. Out of nowhere a guy showed up and pulled him out. That guy said he'd driven the road dozens of times and never stopped, never even thought of stopping, especially not at that particular spot. But that afternoon he stopped. He said it was like somebody made him do it." Tiffany's eyes didn't leave me. "I used to joke that nothing could take Brad until he was good and ready."

I swallowed and felt tears burn my eyes. "Those were major miracles. But that Saturday he didn't need a big miracle. All he needed was to jump off the tractor before it rolled. Just jump," I repeated. "He was a good athlete. He didn't need extra strength. He didn't need extra coordination. All he had to do was jump." I paused. "Without getting his bootlace caught on the clutch pedal," I added huskily. "Was that too much of a miracle to ask for?"

"Maybe those other miracles were for us," Tiffany said gently. "Maybe the miracles that kept Brad here were just postponements that gave *us* borrowed time. If you could choose between never knowing Brad, which would mean you wouldn't hurt now, or having him these last nineteen years, what would you choose?" I stared at her without answering. "Our borrowed time is up," she finished softly. "I don't believe there was any early frost for Brad. He was at peace with himself. He was ready to go, and he didn't go early. Maybe it was early for us, but not for him. You want him to keep running his race, but his race is over. It was a sprint, not a marathon. You have to let him go, Chris." She hesitated. "You keep hanging on, trying to hold him back, and all the while, you're the one that's dying. He's gone, Chris. Have you even been to his grave so that you can see that, so that you can let him go?"

"I don't need to see his grave to know he's gone," I said huskily. "Every morning when I see his empty bed, I know that."

"Chris, maybe you do need to see his grave. Maybe letting go for good is a race that will make a difference for you. It's shorter than a marathon, but maybe it's a lot harder. Maybe that's why you're afraid to run it."

Tiffany stood, brushed at the wrinkles on the front of her blouse, and shrugged. "Roberta and I are leaving in a bit. Are you sure you don't want to come?" I shook my head. She smiled, shrugged, and playfully tapped my shin with her foot. "All right. Your loss. But don't run any races without me."

I stayed in the backyard another twenty minutes before stiffly pushing myself to my feet and shuffling back to the house. Deciding to take a drive, I put on a pair of pants and some shoes and drove the pickup through Eden and Liberty and up the narrow winding road that went over the mountain to North Ogden. A quarter mile from the summit, I pulled off to the side of the road and climbed from the truck.

For a few minutes I surveyed the valley, feeling strangely detached; then my gaze passed over Eden's town cemetery. I ignored it at first, consciously choosing to study other things in the valley, but finally my gaze gravitated back to that spot, and intuitively I understood what Tiffany had tried to tell me—I had to go there to find closure.

I procrastinated as long as I could, but eventually I climbed back into the truck and started down the mountain. I turned off the road onto the paved entrance to the cemetery and parked the truck just inside the driveway leading up the hill to the cemetery itself, choosing to walk the rest of the way, wanting to take my time. I closed the truck door gently, quietly, so as not to disturb the peace and stillness.

The Eden cemetery was miniature, more like a family plot than a community one. It wasn't more than a half acre with fewer than seventy or eighty grave markers, most of them small and simple.

A four-foot-high chain-link fence surrounded the tiny cemetery. Within the fence was trimmed lawn. Immediately outside the fence were weeds, grass, and grazing cattle. On the west side of the cemetery were three Douglas firs, standing as silent sentinels on this quiet, flat-topped hill overlooking the northernmost end of Pineview Reservoir.

I stood alone amid the cold, silent headstones, each one telling its own private history of the individual lying beneath it, and offered a quick, pleading prayer. Since Brad's death my prayers had gravitated toward the short and the rote. This prayer, though short, was full of sincere supplication. I didn't know what I needed, but I desperately wanted to believe God did.

I wasn't exactly sure where Brad's grave was, just the general location—in the vicinity of Grandpa's and Grandma's resting places, which were on the far southeast corner of the cemetery. As I limped across the well-kept grounds, weaving in and around the headstones, I periodically paused and read the stone inscriptions.

"Franklin Gordon McDaniels," I read aloud, "1894 to 1979." I paused and figured—eighty-five years, an old man. He had lived his life to its fullest. I continued to read the inscription aloud. "Husband, father, grandfather, friend. Returned home to the God who gave him life." I didn't remember Franklin Gordon McDaniels. He had died when I was young, but those few simple words on his headstone captured a whole history. There were no regrets, no emptiness, no fractured dreams implied in those words. Franklin Gordon McDaniels's life was over.

I found other similar stories. There were Lindsays, Ferrins, Pritchetts, Johnsons, and more. Then my eyes spotted another—a small stone slab, rising only a few inches above the cut grass. *Melanie Ward Layton, May 4, 1942–December 22, 1969.* I did the same quick calculation in my head as I had done for Franklin McDaniels and others, but the arithmetic added up to tragedy. Twenty-seven years old, and forever gone. The cryptic tale continued, carved in the smooth, white marble: *Loving wife and mother.* The names of four girls followed: *Karen, Susan, Rebecca, and Megan.*

I was about to move on when I spotted a second, much smaller, white marble headstone next to the first. The words written there finished the tale: *Megan Layton, born December 22, 1969, died December 22, 1969. Precious baby gone to God with Mother.*

Death had left a gaping hole in the lives of three young girls and a nameless husband. For a moment I pondered, wondering where Karen, Susan, and Rebecca were. All of them were older than I was, and I had never heard of them. Apparently they had lived in Eden but had moved away. Was their mother's death the cause? Did they even remember their mother, or had they been too young and therefore cheated of the memory, too, or perhaps spared the pain of her passing?

As I wandered among those silent markers and read their simple stories, I at first considered the individuals lying there; but as I continued my quiet trek, more and more my thoughts and questions left the deceased and concentrated on the living they had left behind. Where were they? How did they cope? How often did they reflect upon their missing loved ones? What regrets remained? How long had the pain persisted?

Then I was there. Standing at the head of a new grave. The four-by-eight-foot section of cut sod was a bit dry and burned but beginning to take root again. There was no headstone, only a metal marker, five inches by eight inches. Temporary. When the ground settled, the headstone would replace it. The story written here was incomplete. The only thing I read from its cold metal face were the black block letters on a silver background: *Bradley Grant Huish*.

I had expected more of a shock, but standing there at Brad's grave and looking down at the recently laid sod seemed natural. He was gone. And he wasn't in this place, nor were any of the others who had been laid to rest here over the years. I took comfort in that.

As I stood by Brad's grave, emotions welled inside me. Earlier I had decided that I wouldn't shed more tears, but tears came, and I didn't attempt to hold them back. I was surprised, however, that instead of experiencing bitterness and remorse, I experienced a purging. Standing there alone in the cemetery, I felt a strange peace, a reassuring resolution.

Stuffing my hands into my pockets, I gazed out across the congregation of gray and white headstones, and then my gaze returned to Brad's quiet resting place. Brad had had a good life. It had been short, but it had been one filled with happiness and adventure—and eventual peace with himself and the world around him. And he was now happy, happier than he would have ever been in Mexico or in Eden or in any other place. For a moment I was envious. Envious of Brad! I smiled ruefully, considering the irony.

"I'm sorry, Brad," I whispered, dropping down on my haunches and reaching out to touch the metal marker. I recalled again my harsh words to him, my feelings of jealousy and anger in the garden. I swallowed hard and whispered, "Maybe I'm sorry for me." I closed my eyes a moment. When I opened them, I straightened the marker and rose to a standing position. "I never expected to do this alone, Brad. I'd always planned on us living the rest of our lives together." I took a deep breath, gazing out toward the reservoir's blue water.

Slowly I turned and started away. At first my steps were sluggish and tentative, but then I quickened my pace, as much as my soreness and stiffness allowed. I cut across the cemetery, heading directly toward the truck at the front gate, this time not pausing to study the headstones. I knew I was satisfied—not completely healed, but satisfied that I had gone to the grave and that there was nothing left for me there.

Reaching the truck, I stopped with my hand on the door handle; then another impulse came. There was one more place I needed to visit. One more short race. And this one was mine. I shuddered at the thought, but I was determined. It would be easier now than later.

* * *

The garden was less than three-quarters of a mile from the cemetery. Even though I was stiff and a bit tired, I decided to leave the truck and walk. I started down the road and then cut into the fields, climbing through fences and jumping ditches.

I reached the plank bridge over the irrigation canal and glanced down at the water. I thought of the garden, now a graveyard littered with brown and withered vines no longer needing water. A wave of regret rushed over me; I wished the garden were still a green oasis hidden among the brush-covered ridges, but the hours of work, the sweat and the planning, had been sacrificed to my anger and then negligence.

I started cautiously, almost hesitantly, down the trail to the spot where the tractor had rolled. I dreaded the memories that would flood back, the memories I had struggled to block out. Now I was deliberately going back, permitting myself to remember the horror I had told no one about.

When I arrived, I saw the distinct impressions in the soft dirt made by the tread of the huge tractor wheels. The bank of dirt that had collapsed under the weight of the tractor and had dammed the ditch had been cleared away.

I walked stiffly down the steep embankment and looked about me. The ditch bottom wasn't all that far down from the dirt lane running parallel to it—just a few feet, but enough to turn the awkwardly balanced tractor on its top.

Just as at Brad's grave, I was surprised that I wasn't shocked by this spot. I had dreaded coming here, but now, for some unexplained reason, I felt an enigmatic solace.

Wincing from the pain and stiffness in my legs, I sank down on the side of the bank a few feet from where Brad had taken his last breath. I studied the spot for a moment; then the doors of my memory gradually opened, and the rest of the story—the part I didn't want to remember—came flooding back.

"Brad, give me fifteen minutes. You can hang on that long."

He grabbed for my arm and missed. I moved my hand closer to his and he clasped it tightly. His face was an ashen gray, and big beads of sweat dampened his brow and upper lip. He took a couple of breaths, but I could see that the pressure along his back prevented him from filling his lungs.

I looked around, wishing desperately for help, but there was none. I had to leave him. He still held my hand, his fingers digging into me as he fought back the pain. "It hurts," he gurgled, trying to keep his face out of the dirt. I tried to peel back his fingers to escape his iron grip.

"I don't think it's going to matter, Chris. I've been feeling it ever since . . ." He grimaced and gulped. "As soon as the tractor started to roll, I knew it was over. It all flashed in my mind just like that. I've been feeling it for . . . days." His tongue moved across his lips, and he spat. He had dirt and dust on his face and mouth. "Stay with me, Chris."

Brad saw the water first. "Chris, the water's coming," he groaned.

Even when I looked and saw the first slow trickle of water wrap around my knees as I knelt in the soft dirt next to Brad, I didn't realize what it meant. It was just a minor distraction, something else that was going to make getting Brad out more inconvenient, more uncomfortable.

I stood, and my feet sloshed in the muddy water coming faster now. It was then that panic gripped my insides with a cold, iron fist. When the tractor had tumbled into the ditch, it had brought down the entire west bank with it, and now the tractor and the caved-in dirt formed a dam across the irrigation ditch. At the same time the head-gate at the canal was open, sending down a steady, relentless stream. Already the side of Brad's face was touching the edge of the rising pool.

Dropping to my knees, I lifted Brad's head. "I'm going to shut the water off," I reassured him frantically.

"It's no good, Chris." His eyes went to the huge pile of dirt damming the ditch.

"I'll push the dirt back and let the water run through." Even as I spoke the words, I could see that there was too much dirt to move before the full flood arrived. Within minutes, this entire ditch was going to be full of water, two to three feet deep, and Brad was going to be pinned in the bottom of it.

I attacked the loose dirt with my bare hands, digging and clawing with a wild frenzy. It was no use. I could see that immediately. I had to cut off the water. It was Brad's only hope.

"I'm going to close the headgate," I shouted, slopping back to Brad's side, where he was struggling to keep his face out of the rising water. Brad gripped my hand and pulled me down. "Don't leave me, Chris," he rasped, fighting against the pain and the panic. He swallowed and ran his tongue across his lips. "There's nothing you can do but stay with me."

I glanced desperately up the ditch and knew he was right. There were five to ten minutes of water still coming even if I shut the headgate that very instant. "I'll make it, Brad. I will."

He clung to me and shook his head. Already the water was lapping about his lips and nose, and when he spoke his breath blew little ripples across the muddy water. "I'm not going to make it. But Chris, I couldn't have asked for a better brother. I love you."

I peeled his fingers off my arm. "Keep your face out of the water," I panted, desperate. Even as I said the words, the water was rising toward Brad's mouth and nose. And the water was rushing full force down the ditch now. I had to stop the flow, and yet I had to break through the dam too—do them both at the same instant. But there was no time and no possibility.

"Chris!" Brad called to me, splashing the water wildly as he reached for me. Already he had to blow the water from his mouth as he tried to speak, barely keeping his lips above the waterline. "Chris, take my hand. Talk to me."

Dropping to my knees beside him, I grabbed his flailing hand and pressed it to my face as I bent over him. "Brad, I've got to do something."

He shook his head in the water. He looked at me, our faces inches apart. Through his pain and fear, his thin, pale lips twitched at the corners and he forced out a smile. "I'm sorry, Chris. There are so many . . ." He swallowed and blew the water from his mouth. I raised his head a little farther with my free hand. "So many things I would . . ." He tried to press on but failed. He tried to keep his eyes riveted to mine and away from the wet monster sucking him down. "You'll have to run that marathon without me." He swallowed, ran his tongue over his trembling lips, and coughed.

I was crying now—not just shedding tears, but bawling like a little kid. "I'll get you out, Brad."

I started pulling away from him, but he held on to me for just a moment. "Chris," he called out, beginning to gurgle in the brown water, "I'm not afraid. I'm going to . . ." He choked on the water and suddenly released me. "Now go on," he encouraged. "Get help."

Even as he said those last words, we both knew help wouldn't come in time. He didn't want me to stay and watch the end.

I pulled my hand away and sloshed through the water and up the bank. All the way up the trail to the canal, I stumbled and fell, blubbering and bawling and wiping my tears as I raced.

I prayed with a desperation I'd never experienced. With all my heart I pleaded for divine intervention that would somehow avert Brad's tragic end. Imploring God, I bargained with everything I owned or hoped to achieve. I even offered to trade my life for Brad's.

When I reached the headgate, I hammered it down and heard a tractor in the distance. Looking around, I spotted Winston Howard cultivating a field of corn a half mile away. Leaping a barbed-wire fence and tearing my pant legs and knee as I did, I charged across the field, screaming and waving my hands until Winston stopped, shut off his tractor, and came toward me, seeing and hearing my agonized panic.

"Brad's hurt bad! The tractor rolled on him! Go get help!" Turning, I raced back to where I had left Brad.

When I returned to the overturned tractor, the water was already spilling over the dam and around the tractor, running toward the garden. This wonderful water that had meant life to the garden now meant death to Brad.

I couldn't bring myself to look into the dark pool that had formed behind the tractor. I suppose I wanted to believe that if I didn't see Brad, perhaps the inevitable wouldn't happen. Perhaps, even lying in the water, he could hold his breath for a time. Or if I pulled him out soon enough, I could revive him.

Fetching the one shovel that we had left at the top of the garden, I attacked the mound of dirt, clawing and scooping and burrowing, hoping to break through and release the flood. I don't know how long I worked, but the minutes melted into a horrible blur of anguish. All the while I sensed that I was crying and moaning, and at the same time I called out occasional words of encouragement to Brad.

I was utterly exhausted when I finally broke through the wall of dirt and a trickle of black water seeped out. I dug more desperately, and momentarily a gush washed over me, covering me from the waist down as I knelt in the soft mud.

"I did it!" I shouted. I continued to work like a madman. I didn't stop shoveling until the water flow slowed, and then I dropped the shovel and for the first time since returning to the scene, I peered over and around the tractor, looking for Brad.

There were still a few inches of water behind the dam. At first I didn't see him, and I had a sudden surge of wild hope that perhaps, after the water had softened the ground, he had managed to squeeze out from under the tractor and crawl to safety. And then, in the growing shadows of the deepening dusk, I saw the horrible outline. He was still there, covered by a thin film of brown mud, his head face-down and half submerged in the remaining water.

I crawled down into the water to where he lay. I touched his lifeless shoulder with the tips of my fingers. Shutting my eyes, I buried my head in my arms and wept.

Everything else disappeared into a swirl of fragmented scenes. Dad came, soon followed by Winston and other neighbors. It was over an hour before the men were able to finally lift the tractor enough to pull Brad out. I didn't watch that final stage. By then I had gone to the garden, locked in a numbing daze.

CHAPTER FIFTEEN

I pulled slowly from the memory. Shadows surrounded me as I now sat on the ditch bank, the sun dropping steadily. Hanging my head, I closed my eyes. A few birds sang. A squirrel chattered from the brush. I heard the low buzz of a bee and then the distant hum of an engine over the ridge. A gentle, warm breeze rustled around me, flipping the ends of my hair and brushing my face with its featherlike softness. I could smell the grass, the flowers, and the trees, and felt as though this secluded spot were gently absorbing me.

It seemed strange that the two spots I had dreaded most, where four weeks earlier I had suffered such helplessness and agony, could now assuage the pain and proffer me reassuring peace. Even though regrets lingered, I didn't want to leave this place. I wished that on the last evening of Brad's life I had not succumbed to jealousy, anger, and selfishness. I was ashamed for begrudging Brad anything, even Tiffany, but even as I squirmed from the sting of my own regrets, a calming reassurance helped me realize that Brad would have understood rather than condemned me.

As I had fought for his life, he had certainly known that I loved him. I didn't have to grow the garden to prove that to him. I didn't have to run a marathon for him. After so many years together, Brad knew how I felt about him. Now the Spirit warmed my heart and comforted my mind that the time would come when I'd have the chance to tell and show him again. Heaving a sigh, I opened my eyes and looked around.

"Do you always sit in ditches and wait for beautiful girls to come by?"

I literally jumped and whipped around. Tiffany stood above me dressed in a pair of faded, blue-bib overalls, boots, a long-sleeved orange shirt, and her black Raiders cap. Her hands were pushed into her pockets, and she looked like a regular Daisy Mae. She grinned at me and brushed a strand of hair from her eyes.

"I certainly wasn't expecting to find you here," she commented, cocking her head to one side. "What gives?"

I steadied myself and then trudged stiffly up the bank to the trail. "I wasn't expecting to run into you either," I replied as she extended her hand and pulled me up the last step. "What happened to your movie with Roberta?"

She pulled her hat off and fanned her face. "I decided to look for you," she teased, looking away. "You're a hard one to track down. I didn't think I'd need to come all the way out here to find you." She glanced at me out of the corner of her eye and smiled.

It was then that I noticed the trickle of water in the ditch bottom, the last thing I expected. Startled and staring incredulously, I glanced up the ditch and saw more water coming. "Somebody turned the water on!" I blurted out.

Tiffany laughed and shoved me. "If you weren't such a lazy bum, you would have turned it on yourself. It's our water turn, you know." She put her hat back on. "That's why I didn't go to Salt Lake. I remembered I had irrigation." She smiled. "And since you've been so stingy with your help the last few weeks, you can give me a hand." She squeezed my hand before starting down the trail to the garden.

Puzzled, I followed her down the trail and around the final bend. The garden stretched before me, but rather than brown, withered vines bleaching on the ground, a different scene had been resurrected in its place—a lush, thick, rolling carpet of pale green watermelon vines stretching from one side of the garden to the other, just as I had imagined when I dared to believe that, right here in the valley, we could grow watermelons.

"I don't believe it," I muttered, approaching the rows of vines.

"Touch them and make sure that this isn't some fantastic mirage," Tiffany suggested, laughing. "Go ahead, check them out. They're real."

I reached down and brushed my hands through the vines, parting them periodically. Without hardly trying, I found small, dull green, striped melons.

"Some are softball size," Tiffany explained behind me. "There's one out there in the middle the size of a small football. The weather's been great, so they've really taken off."

I turned and studied the head ditches that I had destroyed. They had been repaired and were now filling with brown water. I turned back to the garden. I had expected it to be dead, but it was teeming with life. This tiny spot had survived and now thrived.

"Is this your work?" I asked, turning to Tiffany, who smiled at my shocked surprise.

"*Our* work—yours and mine and Brad's." She surveyed the garden and then added, "I couldn't just watch it go to waste." Sheepishly pushing her hands into her pockets again, she rocked back and forth on the heels and balls of her feet. "I put a few hours of work down here myself. I've got an investment in this garden, you know. I couldn't turn my back on it." She walked over to where I stood and followed my gaze out across the garden. "Of course, it was never as fun working here alone."

I smiled and then laughed, shaking my head. "It's a miracle. I mean, it's a regular miracle. I figured this place was dead. I wasn't even planning to come down here because I knew what I was going to see and I didn't want to see it." I swallowed, wanting to laugh but feeling an emotional lump in my throat. "And now I come to find that the garden is alive. That last frost didn't get it?"

"Your Grandpa Huish must have cast some weird spell on this place, because nothing down here in the garden was touched."

I glanced over at her. She smiled back. "Thanks, Tiffany," I said quietly. "Brad would have loved this."

She smiled plaintively and looked away. "I didn't do it for Brad. I never did it for Brad." She hesitated. "I did it for you," she added quietly.

"But I thought—"

"Chris Huish, don't you dare give me that junk about me marrying Brad," she cut me off.

I smiled and shrugged. "So . . . ?"

"Chris, I told you that I stopped dreaming about that a long time ago, when I realized I liked somebody else. Somebody who was always there for me." She shook her head in frustration.

Was she serious? I wondered. Had I misread her? "But it's just that . . ." I stammered. I swallowed and wet my lips. "You were there at the garden that last Saturday so you could be with Brad. I just assumed that . . ."

Tiffany inhaled deeply and then exhaled slowly. "That day I came here looking for you. After the night before, I knew how I felt about you. I had suspected for a long time, but when you . . ." She wet her lips. "When you kissed me, I knew."

"But you . . ." I coughed. "You told Brad that you'd go to the dance with—"

"That's because you didn't ask me." Her words spilled out in a rush. "I was waiting. I'd given a ton of hints, and since you hadn't asked and Brad did, I told him I'd go. You were the one I wanted to go with, but you just stood there like a dummy and didn't speak up, so I left. What was I supposed to do, ask you after Brad asked me?"

Hesitantly, I reached out and touched her hand. She didn't respond at first. I took her hand in mine and held it. Still gazing out over the garden, she moved closer to me until our arms and shoulders touched. I released her hand and put my arm around her waist and pulled her close to me. She leaned against me, putting her head against my shoulder and chest, knocking her cap to the ground. Slowly I turned her so she was facing me, and I put my arms about her and pulled her close.

"Tiffany," I whispered, "I don't know if . . ." I paused. "I've never been good about saying how I feel, but I want you to know . . . Tiffany, maybe I don't understand all there is to know about love, but I'm sure that's what I feel right now. I've felt it for a long time. I just thought that you were Brad's, that I could never . . ."

Tiffany smiled at me, her face inches from mine. "You never were very perceptive."

I leaned forward and pressed my lips to hers. "Thanks for being here for me," I said huskily. "Thanks for helping me understand." I took her face between both my hands and studied her. "Why didn't you explain all of this to me before I ran that stupid race this morning?" I smiled. "Maybe you could have talked me out of it and saved me a lot of pain."

"You had to figure all of that out by yourself."

I kissed her again. "Maybe I shouldn't be doing this," I said, a little embarrassed, my cheeks coloring. "Maybe you were planning to save your first kiss for that one real special guy." I smiled.

Tiffany kissed me back. "How do you know I didn't?"

"I still have my mission. That's a race I need to run, one I want to run."

"And I want you to run it." She smiled and kissed me again.

I turned back to the garden with one arm still around Tiffany. Thirty feet from us, I spotted a place where the water had broken through one of the furrows and was beginning to flood. "We better talk later and do something right now about this water, or we're not going to have any watermelons." I looked around. "Did you think to bring a shovel?"

She pointed to a shovel she had left leaning against the juniper tree. I grabbed the shovel and started working frantically to repair the furrow and send the water down the rows of watermelons. The two of us tromped about in the mud, laughing and teasing one another. Then, as always seemed to happen, I inadvertently splashed water on Tiffany as I was repairing a section of ditch. She gasped and glared playfully in my direction. "You did that on purpose."

Holding the shovel with one hand and holding up the other one, I proclaimed my innocence. "It was an accident. I wasn't even—"

Before I could finish, she bent down and slapped a spray of water in my direction. "Now we're even," she declared smugly.

"Even?" I retorted indignantly. "Mine was an accident. That was deliberate." Using the shovel, I splashed a sheet of muddy water in her direction. The water fight was on.

We did manage to give the entire garden a good soaking, but in the process we both came away from the experience dripping and pocked with splotches of mud. We stood side by side at the top of the garden and surveyed the results of our work. Even after all the turmoil and anxiety that this spot had created, at that moment I felt such peace and tranquility that I felt like counting my blessings. "You know, Tiffany," I said softly, becoming serious, "I dreaded coming here. I didn't want to see this place again." I reached out and took her hand. "Now I don't want to leave it."

She smiled. "It's beautiful and peaceful here." She sighed deeply and added, "And it's given us more than watermelons."

We stood there for a long time without speaking, just drinking in the solace and beauty. The sun had disappeared, leaving only a dull, golden glow on the horizon and shadows blanketing the tiny valley. I squeezed Tiffany's hand. "Unless we want to stumble around in the dark, we better head for home." Turning, we started up the trail.

EPILOGUE

That August Tiffany and I harvested our crop of watermelons. We didn't make thousands of dollars; in fact, we barely made nineteen hundred. But by then I was getting ready to leave on my mission to Uruguay, and the money didn't seem to matter very much.

The day I entered the MTC, I missed Brad all over again because there had been a time when I had dreamed about the two of us doing our missions together—not to the same place, but at least at the same time. But then I realized that my dream hadn't been all that far off the mark: we were going to do our missions together—to different places, maybe, but we were running different races.

A year earlier Brad had predicted that life would never be the same for us. He was right. After his death, I never felt the same about the valley. When Brad died there, for me a huge chunk had been carved from the valley's heart and soul. The changes didn't stop there, either. By the time I returned from Uruguay, the Gibsons had moved from Eden. And their moving created another race, one I entered and won. And now, a dozen years after leaving Uruguay, I still run, much as I did on that June morning long ago, with Tiffany by my side, helping me to believe that I will finish the race.

ABOUT THE AUTHOR

Alma Yates was born in Brigham City, Utah, and raised on a small farm just outside of town. From 1970 to 1972, he served as an LDS missionary in the West Mexico Mission. Later he attended Weber State College and BYU, graduating from BYU with a major in English and later with a master's degree in educational administration. After teaching English for seven years, he moved into school administration. Currently he is the principal of Highland Primary School in Snowflake, Arizona.

Alma began writing professionally while he was attending BYU. Since that time he has published several articles in the *Ensign* and *New Era*. Dozens of his short stories have been published in the *New Era*, the *Friend*, and several short-story collections. *Race to Eden* is Alma's eighth novel. He is married to Margery Nadine "Nicki" Cluff, and they are the parents of seven sons and one daughter.